A Quiver of Longing
Trembled through Her

His head bent toward her, and she knew that he was going to kiss her. The tips of his fingers rested lightly along her jaw and the curve of her throat, holding her motionless without any pressure.

The first brush of his lips was soft and teasing, but they came back to claim her mouth with warm ease.

Her lips were clinging to his by the time he finally drew back a few inches to study the result. Slowly her lashes lifted to show the dazed uncertainty in her eyes. She glanced at his face, then lowered her gaze . . .

"Good night, Rev . . . Seth," Abbie murmured.

Books by Janet Daily

The Glory Game
The Pride of Hannah Wade
Silver Wings, Santiago Blue
Calder Born, Calder Bred
Stands a Calder Man
This Calder Range
This Calder Sky
For the Love of God
Foxfire Light
The Hostage Bride
The Lancaster Men
Mistletoe & Holly
Separate Cabins
Terms of Surrender
Night Way
Ride the Thunder
The Rogue
Touch the Wind

Published by POCKET BOOKS

For the Love of God

Janet Dailey

PUBLISHED BY POCKET BOOKS NEW YORK

POCKET BOOKS, a division of Simon & Schuster, Inc.
1230 Avenue of the Americas, New York, N.Y. 10020

Originally published by Silhouette Books.

ISBN: 0-671-55460-3

First Pocket Books printing March, 1985

10 9 8 7 6 5 4 3

POCKET and colophon are registered trademarks
of Simon & Schuster, Inc.

Printed in the U.S.A.

For the
Love of
God

Chapter One

The wind blowing through the opened car window held all the heat and humidity of a July day. It lifted the auburn-gold hair that lay thickly about Abbie Scott's neck, creating a cooling effect. A pair of sunglasses sat on the dashboard, looking at her with their wide, oval lenses. She had removed them earlier, not wanting the view artificially tinted.

A morning shower had brought a sharpness and clarity to the landscape of the Arkansas Ozarks. There was a vividness to the many shades of green in the trees and bushes crowding close to the highway. The air was washed clean of its dust, intensifying the lushness of the Ozark Mountain greenery.

Her hazel eyes kept stealing glances away from the winding roadway to admire the ever-changing vista of rock and tree-covered hills. The flecks of green in her eyes almost seemed like a reflection of the verdant countryside.

There was a time when Abbie hadn't appreciated the beauty around her, when she had complained about the twisting, turning double-lane roads that snaked through the Ozark hills and the lack of entertainment and shopping facilities found in cities, and the limited job opportunities in an area where the major industry was tourism.

Out of high school, Abbie had left the serenity of the rugged hills for the excitement of Kansas City. She thought she'd found it in the beginning, but the glitter had eventually faded. A year ago, Abbie had returned to her hometown of Eureka Springs after four years away.

A lot of people, her parents included, hadn't understood why she had given up a promising career with Trans World Airlines, headquartered in Kansas City, with its many travel and fringe benefits. Abbie's response, if anyone asked, and few did, was a declaration of homesickness. But that was only partially true.

She guessed that her mother suspected a man was at the root of her decision to return, but Abbie had too much pride to admit the romance she thought would lead to the altar had ended up going nowhere. Initially she had come home to lick her wounds, but a year's distance had enabled her to see it had only been the final straw and not the ultimate cause.

Now, instead of a lucrative job with a large corporation, she was her father's legal secretary, paid only a small salary compared to her previous wages. By watching her pennies, Abbie managed fairly well with some adjustments from her prior life-style. She "semilived" with her parents, which meant that she had taken her savings and fixed up the loft above the garage, once a carriage house, into a small efficiency apartment. It provided privacy, as well as low rent.

And there was Mabel—her car. She had traded in her speedy little Porsche sports car for a cheaper and older automobile. Mabel, as Abbie had dubbed the car, wasn't much to look at. Her body was showing signs of rust and dented fenders. She was accidentally two-toned blue, since the hood and the passenger door didn't match the sun-faded robin color of the rest of the car. If it was possible for vehicles to have a personality, Mabel certainly did. She was grumpy, did a lot of coughing and complaining like an old woman, but there wasn't a sick piston or plug in her body.

As the road began an uphill climb, Abbie shifted the standard-transmission car into second gear. The motor made a small grunting sound of protest but Mabel didn't hesitate. Abbie's lips curved with a faint smile.

Although July marked the height of the Ozark tourist season, there was relatively little traffic on the state highway leading into Eureka Springs. Most of the tourists used the major highways, so Abbie only had local traffic to contend with. Plus, it was the middle of a Saturday afternoon, which meant most of the tourists were at the various area attractions and few were on the road.

After experiencing city rush-hour traffic, Abbie didn't let crowded Ozark roads stop her from visiting her grandmother on the weekends. Grandmother Klein continued to live on the rocky farm she and her late husband had worked, although the acreage itself was now leased to a neighbor.

Abbie's grandmother on her mother's side still raised chickens, had a milk cow and a big garden, and canned more food than she could eat, totally ignoring the fact she was seventy years old and should slow down. No one ever visited Grandmother Klein without being loaded down with foodstuffs when they left, and no amount of protesting changed that.

On the floorboard in front of the passenger seat, Abbie had jars of pickles—sweet, dill, bread-and-butter, and cherry—as well as an assortment of homemade preserves and jellies. Plus there were two sacks on the seat. One contained tomatoes, cucumbers, and sweet corn from Grandmother Klein's garden; the other was filled with ripe peaches freshly picked from the tree, their fruity smell filling the car.

The temptation was too much to resist and Abbie reached into the sack for just one more peach as the car neared the crest of the hill. The fruit was still warm from the sun, its juice spurting with the first bite Abbie took. She had to use the side of her hand to keep it from running down her chin.

When she started to sink her teeth into the fuzzy skin for another bite, she saw the red warning light gleaming on the dashboard panel. She lowered the peach from her mouth and frowned slightly. It was rare for Mabel to over-heat on these up-and-down roads.

"Don't lose your cool now, Mabel," she murmured to the car. "We're nearly to the top."

But the light stayed on even after they started the downhill run. When Abbie saw the wisps of steam rising from the hood, she knew there was trouble, and started looking for a place to pull off the road. It was another half-mile before she found a shoulder wide enough to accommodate Mabel. By then, there were more than wisps of steam coming from the hood.

Once the car was parked, Abbie made a quick glance to be sure her lane of the highway was clear of traffic before climbing out to check under Mabel's hood. She forgot she had the peach in her hand until she needed both of them to unlatch the hood. She held it in her mouth, ignoring the juice that dripped onto her blue plaid blouse.

The tails of her blouse were tied at the midriff in an attempt to beat the summer heat. When Abbie started to lift the hood, drops of scalding hot water were sprayed over the band of bare stomach between her blouse and faded Levi's. She jumped back, nearly dropping the peach, and just managing to save it while she wiped the hot water from her stomach with her other hand.

"How could you spit on me like that, Mabel?" she unconsciously scolded the car.

The upraised hood unleashed a billow of steam that quickly dissipated. Abbie moved cautiously closer to peer inside and find the cause of the spitting hot water. There was a hole in the radiator hose. Her shoulders sagged with dismay.

Abbie turned to look up the road, trying to remember how far it was to the nearest farmhouse. It was another four miles yet to the edge of town, she knew. She wasn't enthused about walking even half a mile in this heat.

A semi tractor-trailer rig zoomed by, its draft sucking at her. Abbie looked hopefully at the oncoming traffic. She knew nearly everyone in the area. Maybe someone would drive by that she knew and she could get a ride into town. Not under any circumstances would she accept a lift from a stranger.

More than a dozen vehicles passed but Abbie didn't recognize any of the drivers. A small handful slowed down when they went by her stalled car, but none stopped. And Abbie made no attempt to flag anyone down either. She took an absent bite of the peach while she debated whether to start walking until she reached the nearest house, where she could telephone her parents, or to wait a little longer.

A low-slung, dark green sports car came zipping around the curve in the road, approaching her parked car from the rear. It immediately slowed down at the sight of the upraised hood. The convertible model car had its top down, but its windshield prevented Abbie from getting a clear view of the man behind the wheel. As it edged onto the shoulder to park behind her car, she noticed the out-of-state license plates and tensed a little. Four years of living in a city had made her slightly leery of strangers.

The driver didn't bother to open the door. Instead, he lightly vaulted over the low side to walk toward Abbie's car. The man was tall, easily reaching the six-foot mark. In this land of the summer tourist, there was nothing unusual about the way he was dressed—a mottled gray T-shirt and faded cutoffs with white sneakers. It exposed an awful lot of hard, sinewy flesh, tanned to a golden brown. His hair was a toasty gold color, attractively rumpled by the wind.

Abbie couldn't see his eyes behind the mirror-like finish of his sunglasses, but she liked the strong angles and planes of his male features. She felt that instant pull of attraction to the opposite sex and experienced a twinge of regret that the man was no more than a passing stranger. There wasn't exactly a surfeit of good-looking, single men in Eureka Springs.

"Hello." His lips parted in a brief but friendly smile that showed an even row of strong white teeth. "It looks like you have some car trouble."

" 'Fraid so," Abbie admitted.

In spite of the futility of it, her interest in the man mounted as he lifted a hand to remove the sunglasses. She found herself gazing into a pair of arresting blue eyes. Their depths held a warm gleam that had a dancing charm all its own. Awareness of his sexual magnetism quivered pleasantly along her nerve ends. It had been a long time since any man had fully aroused her mating interests. The few times she had gone out on a date since her return, the desire had been mainly for companionship.

"What seems to be the problem?" As the stranger bent to look under the hood, Abbie observed the flexing muscles in his tanned arms.

Even though the busted hose had stopped spitting hot water, Abbie still advised, "Be careful. Mabel sprang a leak." The curious glance he slanted at her made Abbie realize she had referred to the car by its pet name. "That's what I call her," she explained lamely, and felt slightly foolish about it.

An interest that had not been present before entered his look as he briefly skimmed Abbie from head to foot. She was tall, nearly five foot seven, with a model's slimness—except she had curves in all the right places, although no one would ever describe her as voluptuous. Her light red hair had a gold sheen to it—strawberry blond her mother called it. Abbie would have been less than honest if she didn't acknowledge she was more than reasonably attractive. A country freshness kept her from being striking.

The stranger seemed to like what he saw without being offensive about it. Then his attention was swinging easily back to the split in the radiator hose. He tested the hose, bending it a little to discover the extent of the rupture.

"I might be able to patch 'Mabel' up." He used

her pet name for the car. The faint smile that edged the corners of his mouth seemed to share —or at least understand—her personification of the car. "Would you happen to have a rag—or an old towel?"

"Sure. I have one under the front seat," Abbie admitted. "Just a second and I'll get it for you."

Rather than use the driver's side with the road traffic to watch for, Abbie walked through the tall grass along the shoulder of the highway and opened the passenger door. It was a long stretch to reach the piece of old flannel tucked under the drivers' seat. Her elbow bumped some of the jars on the floor, rattling them together. Like a row of dominoes, they began toppling over just as her groping fingers found the rag under the seat. Abbie closed her eyes, expecting to hear one of the jars break and bracing herself for the sound, but it didn't come.

The rag was in her hand and she was half lying on the seat, preparing to push out of the car when Abbie heard the swish of footsteps in the grass. There wasn't much room on the seat for maneuvering with the two sacks of vegetables and peaches. Abbie was forced to crane her neck around in an effort to see behind her.

"Are you all right?" The man was standing on the inside of the opened car door, eyeing her with concern.

She was conscious of being in a vulnerable and ungainly position with no graceful way to alter it. "Yes. I just knocked over some jars." She pushed backward off the seat and out of the car. Her face felt red but it could have been caused by the blood rushing to her head when she had been half hanging over the seat to reach the rag.

When Abbie turned to give him the old cloth, she discovered how close she was standing to him. The cotton fabric of the mottled gray T-shirt was cleaved to his wide shoulders and lean, muscled chest. His maleness became a potent force Abbie had to reckon with, especially since she was standing nearly eye level with his mouth. Her pulse just wouldn't behave at all.

"Did you break anything?"

She watched his lips form the words but it was a full second before his question registered. Abbie pulled herself up sharply. What was the matter with her? She was reacting like a love-starved old maid who hadn't been near a man in years. A little voice argued that she hadn't—at least not with a man the caliber of this one.

Her hazel-green eyes darted a guilty look upward to meet his gaze. There seemed to be an awareness in his blue eyes of what she was thinking and feeling. It really wasn't so surprising. Experience with life—and women—was etched into the male lines in his face.

"Nothing was broken." Abbie remembered to answer his question. Her crooked smile held a measure of resignation. "Grandmother Klein loaded me down with her homemade jams and pickles before I left."

His shoulder brushed her forearm as he bent to set the jars upright. With his large hand, he was able to right them two at a time, sometimes with a thumb on the third to push it up. In next to no time, all the jars were standing again.

"Thank you. You really didn't have to do that," Abbie said when he had finished.

He raised his eyebrows in a kind of shrugging gesture. "I remember my grandmother used to make the best wild-raspberry jam. She knew it was my favorite and always made sure to have a couple of jars for me whenever I visited her. Grandmothers are like that. They either try to fatten you up or marry you off."

"That's true," Abbie agreed dryly, and resisted the impulse to look at his left hand to see if his grandmother had succeeded in the latter. "Here's the rag you wanted." She gave it to him and followed when he walked around the opened passenger door to the front of the car. "What are you going to do?" she asked. "Wrap the rag around the hose and use it as a bandage?"

"No." He appeared amused by her suggestion, but not in a ridiculing way. "I doubt if it would hold. I have some electrical tape in my car. Once I get the hose dried off, I'll wrap a few lengths of that around it. It's only a few miles to Eureka Springs, and the tape should hold until you get that far."

Abbie bit her lower lip, remembering. "Except most of the water boiled out of the radiator."

Using the rag as a protective pad, he unscrewed the radiator cap. "I always carry a gallon jug of drinking water with me. Between it and a gallon of antifreeze-coolant in my trunk, we should be able to get you temporarily fixed up."

She shook her head in a gesture of bewildered amazement at how smoothly he was handling the breakdown. "I'm certainly glad you came along," Abbie declared openly. "I thought I was going to have to walk to a phone, and this isn't exactly the coolest day for walking, not to mention the tow charges you're saving me. Thank you for stopping."

"Just being a Good Samaritan," he replied, that easy smile coming again to his mouth.

With the coolant, water, and tape from his car, he patched the hose and partially filled Mabel's radiator. "The old gal ought to make it now," he said as he closed the hood and made sure it was tightly latched.

"It isn't enough to say 'thank you,'" Abbie insisted. "You not only fixed it but you used your tape and water and everything. Let me pay you for it."

He opened his mouth to refuse, then suddenly smiled. It seemed to take her breath away as her heart started thudding crazily. Love wasn't something that happened at first sight but physical attraction could. It was often equally potent, however, and Abbie knew she was suffering from a severe case of it.

"Were those fresh peaches I smelled in the sack on the car seat?" he asked instead.

"Yes." Abbie nodded while she studied the way the afternoon sun intensified the burnished gold color of his hair, antiquing it.

"If you insist on paying me, I'll take a couple of those peaches. Homegrown fruit has a taste all its own," he said.

"Okay, it's a deal." She laughed and walked to the passenger side to retrieve the sack through the opened car window. "Help yourself. You can have the whole sack. Grandmother Klein will just give me more next weekend."

"Two's plenty." He randomly picked two from the sack. "I'll follow you into Eureka Springs to make sure you don't have any more trouble with Mabel. I'll be stopping there, and I advise that you stop at the first garage and get a new hose put on."

"I will." It was a somewhat absentminded agreement, because her attention had been caught by his statement that he'd be stopping at Eureka Springs. "Eureka Springs is a quaint town. Will you be staying there awhile?"

"Yes, I plan to," he admitted, and she was conscious of his gaze running over her again.

"You'll like it," she rushed, only half-aware that he had been going to say something else. As a rule, she didn't socialize with summer tourists. A holiday romance was even more of a dead end than any other kind. But there was no doubt in her mind that she wanted to see this man again. "By the way, my name's Abbie Scott. You've already met Mabel."

"Abbie? Short for Abra?" He arched an eyebrow.

Abbie was dumbfounded. "How did you know that? Most people think my name is Abigail."

One muscled shoulder was lifted in an expressive shrug. "It just seemed appropriate. Abra was the favorite of Solomon in the Bible. A lucky guess." He extended a hand to complete the introductions. "My name's Talbot. Seth Talbot."

"That's a biblical name, too." Abbie was reluctant to admit she hadn't known anything about her namesake. Since he seemed so knowledgeable about it, she didn't want to reveal her ignorance.

"Seth was the third son of Adam," he informed her. "Not quite as well known as his older brothers, Cain and Abel."

"That's true." She smiled. Her hand tingled pleasantly in his firm clasp. He had very strong, capable hands, but they were relatively smooth, without the calluses of someone who made his living with them. It didn't really surprise her. Despite his hard physique and craggy good looks, there was the definite impression of a man who relied on his mental prowess and innate air of command for his living.

Then he was releasing her hand to gather up his empty jugs and roll of black tape. "If you start to have any trouble, just honk twice. I'll be right behind you," Seth Talbot assured her.

"Okay." She watched him walk along the grassy verge to his car and stow the things in the backseat.

Oncoming traffic permitted her to observe him as he swung over the low passenger door and into the driver's seat. Abbie waited until the road was clear to walk to the driver's side of her car and open the door. She set the sack of peaches on the seat and pushed it over to slide behind the wheel.

Mabel's motor grumbled to life at the turn of the ignition key. As Abbie turned the car onto the highway she waved to the driver of the sports car. Within seconds, she saw the reflection of the dark green sports car in her rearview mirror, following a safe distance behind her.

It was an older model car, but Abbie suspected it had been an expensive one. She tried to guess what kind of work he did, speculating that he could be a lawyer or maybe a doctor. If he was a salesman, he could sell her anything, she thought with a little laugh.

The four miles to Eureka Springs seemed to flash by. Not once did Mabel even wink her red warning light. Abbie couldn't make up her mind whether she was glad or sorry about that. Mechanical trouble would have given her an opportunity to find out more about Seth Talbot— essentials like where he was staying in Eureka Springs and some of the places he had planned to see while he was here.

Abbie couldn't believe the way she was thinking. She was actually considering chasing a man. There was nothing shy about her, but she didn't classify herself as the aggressive type either. Still, she couldn't help wondering what it would be like if he kissed her. Seth Talbot had certainly captured her fancy in a short time. Or maybe it was simply a sign that she was finally cured of her distrust for men after that disappointing romance in Kansas City. That was probably closer to the truth.

When Abbie turned her car into the service station-garage she patronized, there was a honk and a wave from the sports car before it sped on by. Abbie couldn't contain the sigh of regret that slipped out. It would be sheer chance if she ever saw him again and she knew it.

A portly, coverall clad man emerged from the service bay of the station and walked toward her car with an ambling gait. It was Kermit Applebaum, the owner of the establishment. He had serviced her parents' vehicles ever since she was a freckle-faced toddler. Thankfully, the freckles had faded with the onset of maturity, but Kermit Applebaum still called her Freckles, a nickname no one else had picked up—and Abbie was eternally grateful for that.

"Well, hello, Freckles," he greeted her as she had expected, and Abbie tried not to wince. "How's old Gladys doing?"

"Her name is Mabel," she corrected patiently, and stepped out of the car. "And Mabel has busted a radiator hose. I hope you have a spare one to fit her."

"I'll rustle up something." He wiped his greasy hands on a rag before he lifted the hood to have a look. "You didn't do a bad job of patchin' this."

"I can't take the credit for that," Abbie replied. "A tourist stopped when he saw I was broken-down and fixed it up for me, then followed me into town to be sure I made it."

"That fella that just honked at you?" the owner-mechanic asked with some surprise. When she nodded affirmatively his expression became thoughtful. "I thought it was just some guy tryin' to make time with you. I guess I did him a disservice." He closed the hood with a decisive shove and turned to Abbie. "Drive your car over to that empty bay, and I'll see what I've got for hoses to fit it."

In all, it took the better part of two hours before he had it fixed with interruptions from customers and phone calls. It was nearly suppertime when Abbie turned her trusty car onto a winding street for home.

Her hometown of Eureka Springs was filled with quaint charm. The restored and refurbished Victorian structures clinging to the steep hills gave the city an ambience of the past, a nostalgic flavor. Some visitors considered it an oddity in the middle of the Ozarks, but Abbie had always regarded it as home. It had been dubbed "The Little Switzerland of America" because of the combination of its architecture and steep terrain and had been a highly popular vacation resort since the turn of the century. Then, its appeal had been as a spa. Now, it was the town itself and its many gift, antique, and craft shops. There was even a trolley car to ease the weary feet of those unprepared for the endlessly winding streets.

And during the tourist season, people came by the thousands to see The Great Passion Play, an outdoor drama of Christ's last days, and to view the seven-story statue of Christ of the Ozarks. There were other religious attractions, too, including the Bible Museum, the Christ Only Art Gallery, and the New Holy Land with its life-size recreations of scenes from the Bible.

As much as Abbie loved her hometown and its picturesque buildings and Ozark Mountain setting, living in a town that had essentially changed little since the turn of the century had its disadvantages. Abbie became as irritated as the next motorist on city streets that were not designed to handle a lot of modern vehicle traffic. And there weren't any traffic lights, which meant relying on the courtesy of another driver in the case of making turns onto main thoroughfares or off of them.

In the summer, when the visitors came by the hundreds, she griped along with everyone else at the traffic tie-ups, but she still loved it. Maybe it was because she was like the town—a little out-of-date and out-of-step with the times— proud and old-fashioned.

All her girl friends were married, and most of them had children. She had given up a promising career and come back to—what? To fantasize about a stranger who stopped to help?

Climbing roses spilled over the fan-shaped trellises that marked the driveway of her parents' home with its gingerbread trim. The old carriage-house-turned-garage sat at the side, literally built into the hill. Her father's car was already inside the garage. Since there was only room for one and the weather couldn't hurt

Mabel's appearance, Abbie always parked outside.

This time she stopped near the back door of the two-and-a-half story white house. Her cupboards were already filled with jars of goods from Grandmother Klein. She knew the elderly woman wouldn't mind if her granddaughter gave some of the food and home-canned goods to the woman's daughter and son-in-law. It certainly made more sense to divide it now than carry it all up a flight of stairs to her apartment, then back down to the house.

Without bothering to knock at the back door, Abbie walked into the kitchen with an armload of jars. The rush of air-conditioned coolness hit her, and she paused to savor the relief from the outside heat.

A tall, auburn-haired woman turned away from the stove where the evening meal was cooking to look at Abbie. There was a definite resemblance between mother and daughter with minor differences. Alice Scott was pencil-thin, with eyes that were more green than hazel. "You and Mother must have had quite a visit today," she remarked. "She isn't ill or anything?"

"No." Abbie walked to the breakfast table and carefully set the jars down. "I busted a radiator hose on the way home. I've been over at Kermit's for the last two hours getting it repaired."

"I don't see what keeps that car together at all," her mother replied with a wry shake of her head.

The unmistakable sound of her father running

down the steps and whistling a tuneless song echoed into the kitchen. In a few things, her father was very predictable. One of them was his routine after a day at the office. He immediately changed into a pair of khaki pants and either a cotton plaid shirt in the summer or a bedraggled maroon pullover sweater in the winter upon coming home from the office.

True to his pattern, he entered the kitchen in the plaid shirt and khaki pants. He sniffed at the food cooking on the stove. "Smells good, honey." He kissed his wife on the cheek and walked to the refrigerator for a beer. "When do we eat?" Then he saw Abbie standing by the table. "I thought we pushed that one out of the nest. Here she is back at mealtime with her mouth open."

"There's plenty," her mother assured her as she turned the sizzling pork chops in the skillet. "Why don't you have supper with us?"

"Not tonight, Mom. Thanks just the same." Abbie refused because it would be too easy to fall into the habit of eating her meals at home. She had become used to living on her own and liked the measure of independence the small apartment above the garage gave her.

"You're too stubborn," her father accused, but he grudgingly admired her streak of independence, too.

"I get it from you," she retorted.

"You can have Sunday dinner with us tomorrow." It wasn't an invitation from her mother; it was a statement. "It will be nice for all three of us to attend church together again."

26

Her father cleared his throat and looked uncomfortable. "Abe said something about going fishing tomorrow. I meant to mention that to you the other day."

"Drew Fitzgerald Scott, you are going to church." Her mother shook a fork at him. "It's the last time Reverend Augustus will be conducting the services. He's retiring."

"Hallelujah!" Her father raised a hand in the air in mock rejoicing.

"Drew." Her mother's voice held a warning note.

"I never did like the man," he reminded her. "I'm not going to be sorry to see him retire. If I go to church with you tomorrow, you can be sure I'll be sitting in that pew rejoicing."

"Not 'if,'" Alice Scott corrected. "You *are* going. And you're going to attend the farewell tea our ladies' club is giving him and Mrs. Augustus tomorrow afternoon."

His glance slid to Abbie, an impish light dancing in his brown eyes. "Are you going?"

"Yes, she's going." Her mother answered for her.

Abbie lifted her shoulders in a shrug that said the decision had been taken out of her hands. "You heard her, Dad." A smile widened her mouth. "I'm going."

"I guess I don't have a choice either," he replied affably, then took a deep, sighing breath. "I just hope we don't get another 'hell and damnation' minister. I like to go to church and be inspired, not threatened." He leaned a hip against the butcher-block table in the middle of the sunny yellow kitchen. "What about it, Mother? What's the word on our new minister?"

Her mother switched off the burner under the skillet and paused. "I don't remember anyone discussing him in specifics, except that he's supposed to be highly qualified." She seemed surprised that her information was so scanty. "But we'll meet him and his family tomorrow. Reverend Augustus will be introducing them to the congregation, and I'm sure they'll attend the tea. You'll be able to draw your own conclusions."

With that subject apparently closed, Abbie had the chance to ask the question that had been buzzing around in her mind since this afternoon. "Mom, what made you choose the name Abra for me? Does it have any special meaning?"

"That's a strange question to ask after all these years," her mother declared with a faint laugh. "One of my girl friends had an aunt by that name and I liked it. Why?"

"I just found out Abra was the name of Solomon's favorite wife in the Bible. I guess I wondered if you had known that." Abbie shrugged.

"How interesting." Her mother looked pleasantly surprised. "Who told you this?"

"A tourist who stopped to help me when Mabel broke down—" Abbie didn't have a chance to complete the sentence in its entirety.

"What's this about Mabel breaking down?" her father interrupted.

And Abbie explained again about the busted radiator hose and her delay getting it fixed at the garage. By the time she had finished answering —or trying to answer—all his mechanical questions, her mother was dishing up their evening meal. Abbie refused a second invitation to join them and left the house to carry the bounty from her grandmother up to her apartment.

Chapter Two

The incessant pounding roused Abbie from her sleep. She rolled over with a groan and buried her head under the pillow, but she couldn't drown it out. Whoever was doing all that hammering should be put in jail for making so much noise on a Sunday morning, she thought.

Sunday morning. There wasn't anyone hammering, she realized. Someone was knocking on her door. Abbie threw aside the pillow and tossed back the covers to sit up in the single bed. The grogginess of sleep blurred her eyes as she grabbed for the robe draped over the foot of the bed.

"I'm coming!" she called while she hurriedly tried to pull on her robe, but she wasn't too coordinated.

Her alarm clock sat on the oak dresser, far enough from the bed so she would be forced to get up to turn it off. Abbie peered at it. The hour hand pointed to one. Sunshine was streaming through the bedroom window. It surely didn't mean it was one o'clock in the afternoon! With a groan she realized the clock had stopped. She must have forgotten to wind it last night.

It was obviously late, but Abbie had no idea what time it was. She hurried through the main room of her loft apartment, which included a living room, dining room, and kitchen, to the staircase door. As she opened it she lifted the weighty mass of auburn-gold hair away from her face.

Her father stood outside, dressed in a suit and tie. His gaze wandered over her while a smile deepened the corners of his mouth. "I don't think that's exactly the proper attire for church," he observed.

"My clock stopped." Abbie didn't mention that she had forgotten to wind it. "What time is it?" Her voice still contained the husky thickness of sleep.

"There's about ten minutes before the church service starts. Is that any help?" he asked with an amused slant to his mouth.

"I can't get ready in five minutes," Abbie groaned. "You and Mother will just have to go without me."

A rueful expression added lines to his face. "She isn't going to be too happy about that," he warned Abbie but not without understanding. "Too bad *I* didn't think of it." A boyish grin showed.

"Mom is your alarm clock," she reminded him. "She would have gotten you up in plenty of time."

A horn honked an impatient summons from the driveway. Her father glanced in the direction of the sound. "Your mother hates to be late. What shall I tell her?" he asked. "Will you be coming later on?"

"The service will be half over by the time I could make it there." Abbie shook her head to indicate she wouldn't be attending church that morning. "You'll have to convey my apologies to Reverend Augustus and assure him that I'll be at the afternoon tea."

"I think I'll let your mother have that pleasure." He began moving away from the door to the white-painted staircase. "See you after church."

With no reason for haste, Abbie took her time in the shower while coffee perked in the kitchen. The warm spray awakened her senses and eliminated the last traces of sleep and she stepped out of the shower feeling refreshed and invigorated. With a towel wrapped around her wet hair, she donned the yellow cotton robe again and ventured into the kitchen area of the apartment.

A counter bar separated the kitchen area from the rest of the room. Although there was a small wooden table and chairs, Abbie usually ate most of her meals at the counter, using the table only when she had friends over for a meal.

It was too close to dinnertime for breakfast, so Abbie settled for a glass of orange juice and a cup of freshly perked coffee, sitting on a tall, rattan-backed stool at the counter-bar. By the time she had drunk a second cup, the towel had absorbed most of the moisture from her hair. It took only a few minutes to finish drying it with the blow dryer. Its natural-bodied thickness assumed a casually loose and free style that curled softly about her neck. Choosing a dress to wear that would be both suitable for the minister's farewell party and comfortable in the July heat was relatively easy, because she had so few choices. Abbie picked out a sundress designed with classic simplicity, a white material with small, navy-blue polka dots. Its neckline was modest, while the close-fitting bodice flattered the thrusting curves of her breasts. A wide leather belt in navy-blue accented her slender waist, with the skirt flaring out to near fullness. Abbie had a pair of navy-blue sandals with stacked, wooden heels to complete the outfit. She had a three-banded bracelet and matching hooped earrings to wear with it for the finishing touch, but Reverend Augustus frowned on jewelry. After debating silently with herself for several minutes, Abbie wore them anyway.

The only clock with the right time was in the kitchen. It warned her that it was nearly time for church to be let out. She crossed the driveway to the house. Unlike Abbie, her parents had never acquired the habit of locking their doors. In this small community, there had never been any reason to worry about it.

Her mother was a terribly organized person. All the preparations for Sunday dinner were completed, from the meat and vegetables baking in the oven to the relish tray and salad sitting in the refrigerator. Abbie went ahead and put the latter on the table, already covered with their best linen tablecloth, china and silverware. There was even a bouquet of freshly cut flowers adorning the center.

When she heard her parents' car turn into the driveway, Abbie tied an apron around her waist and took the roaster from the oven. She was forking the tender roast onto the meat platter when her parents walked in the back door. Abbie sent a smile in their direction.

"How was the service?" she asked brightly, already warned by the disapproving glint in her mother's eye that she was still upset with her for missing church.

"Reverend Augustus gave an excellent farewell sermon. You should have been there, Abbie," her mother stated. Her tone held more disappointment than anger.

"She means it was brief," her father inserted in a teasing fashion. "For once he didn't rant and rave until he was drowned out by growling stomachs."

Her mother took another apron from the drawer and tied it around her middle to help Abbie dish up the food. "His sermon was quite poignant."

"Maudlin," her father declared with a wink at Abbie.

"He did wander a bit," her mother admitted. "But I thought it was just all the more touching."

Abbie turned to her father, going off the subject for an instant. "Are you going to carve the roast?" At his nod, she laid the carving knife and fork across the meat platter. "What is the new minister like?"

"Old Augustus got so choked up with sentimentality he forgot to introduce him." Her father laughed. "I guess he was sitting in one of the front pews but the church was so crowded I never got a look at him. I had the impression that the reverend didn't totally approve of his replacement though."

"Oh?" Abbie gave him a curious look. "Why?"

"I don't know." He admitted his uncertainty. "It was something in his tone of voice when he talked about the church having young blood in its ministry."

"I'm sure that he only meant to imply that the new minister and his family were young people," Alice Scott insisted. "It was merely an oversight that he forgot to introduce the new reverend to the congregation."

"Oversight or not, if Reverend Augustus disapproves of him, I think I'll like him," her father stated.

"You really should show more forbearance, Drew," her mother admonished as she passed him the platter of meat. "Take this into the dining room."

The tea was set for four o'clock in the church basement. Since it was Alice Scott's ladies' club that was giving it for the retiring minister, she had to be there early to help get everything set up. Somehow, Abbie and her father were persuaded to offer their assistance in setting up the rows of folding chairs and the long serving tables.

Abbie was busy setting out the trays of fancy-cut sandwiches when the guests of honor, Reverend Augustus and his wife, arrived in the company of a dozen or so of their closest friends in the church. With the napkins and silverware still to be laid out in a fanning display, Abbie hadn't the time to leave her work to greet them and managed only a brief glance in their direction. After their arrival, people seemed to flood into the large room. Abbie hurried to finish before someone approached the refreshment table.

She was still holding a handful of spoons when she heard footsteps behind her. There was no quick way to arrange so many, so she continued to place them one by one and hoped the person would be patient for a minute or two longer.

"Well, hello, Miss Scott," a man's voice greeted her with warm pleasure. The familiarity of it seemed to tingle through her as her lips parted in a silent breath of delight.

Abbie was so taken by surprise when she recognized the voice of the man, Seth Talbot, who had stopped to help her yesterday, that she didn't even wonder what he was doing at the tea. She swung around to face him.

"Hello, Mr. Talbot." At first her gaze went no farther than his magnetically blue eyes. They seemed sexier than she remembered, so blue against his darkly bronzed features.

Just what drew her attention to his attire, Abbie couldn't have said, because dumb shock set in immediately afterward. She couldn't seem to tear her gaze away from the narrow strip of a white collar that circled his neck, the symbolic garb of an ordained minister.

"Did you get a new hose for Mabel?" he asked.

Abbie heard him but her vocal chords were frozen. All she could do was nod, but his question did succeed in lifting her rounded gaze to his face. Looking at his ruggedly handsome face and darkly gold hair made it seem all the more incredible. There was nothing benign about his countenance, nothing to lead a person to suspect he was a man of God. There was too much virility, too much hard masculinity, too much that suggested male passions.

Something flickered over his expression. "Is something wrong?"

"Yes. No. That is . . ." She stumbled over the words, realizing how rudely she had been gaping at him. Finally, honesty won out. "I never guessed that you were a minister. You don't look like one."

"I see." The corner of his mouth deepened with amusement, attractive lines fanning out from the corners of his eyes.

"I meant . . . yesterday, on the road, you didn't

look like one." She was making a terrible mess of the explanation. "It's obvious by what you're wearing today that you are but . . ." Abbie paused to gather her scattered wits. "I'm sorry."

"For what?" he challenged lightly. "It was a natural reaction. I hadn't realized that you lived in Eureka Springs, or I would have mentioned my transfer to this church."

"But . . ." As her mind played back their previous day's meeting, Abbie discovered that she hadn't mentioned that she lived here. ". . . I guess I didn't tell you."

"I'm glad you're a member of my new congregation." That tantalizing half-smile seemed permanently affixed to his mouth. "I was beginning to think no one under forty belonged to this church."

There was so much potent male charm in that look, Abbie had to glance at his collar to remind herself of his profession. It would be so easy to forget.

"With summer and all, a lot of the members my age have other plans," she said tactfully, rather than criticizing the outgoing pastor for not doing more to encourage the attendance of younger members.

"Maybe you can help me persuade some of them to include Sunday-morning church service in their plans," Reverend Seth Talbot suggested.

All her impulses were to leap on the suggestion, but Abbie seriously questioned whether she was motivated by a desire to help the church or wanted to accept because she was physically attracted to him. She strongly suspected it was the latter. All her responses to him at the moment were purely feminine.

"I'm afraid I'm not a very active church member myself . . . Reverend." Abbie had trouble getting his professional title out. It seemed at such odds with his compelling manhood. She was conscious of the little vein pulsing in her neck.

If he noticed her hesitancy in addressing him, he tactfully ignored it. "Then I'll have to make you my first sheep to win back to the fold." His smile deepened with a heady force.

Abbie lowered her gaze to resist his undeniable appeal. Charisma, that's what it is, she told herself. He would attract anybody's attention—not just hers.

"Abbie, are you finished yet?" Her mother's voice broke into their conversation.

She turned with a guilty start, just as if she were a little girl again getting caught red-handed doing something naughty. It was an expression her mother recognized and it narrowed her gaze. There were still a half-dozen spoons in Abbie's hand. She glanced quickly at them, her task forgotten until that moment. "I'm almost done," she told her mother.

But Alice Scott's attention had already strayed to the man standing next to Abbie. Her eyes widened slightly at the black frock and white collar.

"I don't believe we've met." Seth took the initiative to correct that. "I'm Reverend Talbot, your new pastor."

"I'm sorry." Abbie realized she had forgotten her manners. "This is my mother, Alice Scott."

"I noticed the resemblance," he said, directing that warm, male smile at her mother. "It's easy to see that your daughter inherited her looks from you, Mrs. Scott."

The remark could have sounded so polite and commonplace, a meaningless response, but the way he said it seemed sincere, a glowing compliment. Abbie was a little astounded at the way her mother seemed to blossom under his spell, shedding years and acquiring a youthful beauty. Just for a minute, she was irritated with her mother.

"My father is here somewhere," Abbie informed Seth and glanced around the room in search of him. "But I don't see him this minute." The remark was offered in an unconscious attempt to remind her mother that she was married.

"My husband has been looking forward to meeting you, Reverend Talbot," her mother explained, then inquired, "Is your family here?"

Abbie was suddenly crushed by the idea that Seth already had a wife and children. Seth. She was thinking of him by his first name. That had to stop.

"My family?" An eyebrow quirked, then straightened to its normal line. "You mean my wife? I'm one of the rare ones, Mrs. Scott, an unmarried minister."

"You're a bachelor?" Her mother's tone of voice made it a question, as if she needed more confirmation of his single status.

"Yes." His straightforward answer didn't leave any room for doubts, and Abbie felt a tremble of relief. It was bad enough being so strongly attracted to a minister. It would have been worse if he were married on top of it.

"I wasn't trying to pry, Reverend Talbot," her mother assured him. "But as you said, it is unusual."

"I guess I'm something of a bad boy." He included Abbie in his sweeping glance. "I should be busy choosing a proper minister's wife, but I prefer to wait until I can find the right woman for me—not my job."

"I suspect you are unorthodox in a number of different ways," Abbie murmured, remembering the way he had been dressed the previous day, and the racy sports car he'd been driving.

"So I've been told." There was a wicked light dancing in his eyes. It seemed totally inappropriate for a man of God. There was more than a trace of rebel in him, Abbie realized.

"What do you do when someone tells you that?" she asked.

"I pray on it." Then he addressed himself to her mother. "My way of doing things is sometimes regarded as unconventional, but it doesn't necessarily make it wrong." He seemed to be

41

quietly warning her that his methods wouldn't be the same as those of their previous pastor.

"I'm sure we all have some adjustments to make," her mother conceded smoothly, but there appeared to be reluctant admiration in her look. "I guess we can start out by being thankful that you don't have long hair and a beard."

"You mean like Jesus," he murmured.

Her mother breathed in sharply, then smiled. "You have me there, Reverend Talbot."

"I prefer to have you at church on Sunday mornings," he replied with a silent laugh that slashed grooves in his lean cheeks.

"Our family will be there," her mother promised as her glance strayed beyond him. "Abbie, you'd better finish putting those spoons out. We want to start serving." She seemed to suddenly remember her initial purpose in coming to the refreshment table.

"Excuse me, ladies." He inclined his bronze head in their direction and withdrew.

As Abbie watched him walk away to mingle with the growing crowd, she tried not to notice how becoming he looked in black, and the way the cut of his suit showed off the tapering width of his chest and shoulders. It seemed wrong to be observing those things about him.

"Abbie." Her mother's prompting voice pulled her gaze from his compelling male figure. "Put the spoons out."

"I will." Then she asked, "What do you think of him?"

There was a long pause while her mother's gaze traveled across the room to where he was standing. "I haven't made up my mind," she answered finally.

People were starting to drift toward the refreshment table as Abbie laid the last few spoons out. She helped herself to two cups of coffee from the urn and went in search of her father. One of the cups was for him and the other for herself. Like a magnet, her gaze was drawn to Seth. She forced it to move onward until she spied her father in the far corner of the room, talking to one of his fishing buddies.

It wasn't easy to work her way through the throng of people, carrying two cups of hot coffee, but she made it. Engrossed in his conversation, her father looked startled when she extended the cup within range of his vision. He glanced up.

"Is that for me?" he asked.

"I thought you might have talked yourself dry with all your fish tales," Abbie said.

"There are fish *tales* and there are *fish* tails, get it?" His friend, Ben Cooper, chuckled at his own pun.

Abbie groaned in mock dismay at the poor humor. Ben Cooper had his insurance office next door to her father's law offices, so he was a frequent visitor, dropping in regularly for coffee.

"I'd offer you this cup of coffee, Ben, but it's black and I know you prefer yours drowned in milk," she explained.

"That's all right. I'll get my own." He hitched

the waistband of his suit pants higher around his middle as he stood up. "Save my chair for me, will you, Abbie?"

"Sure." She obligingly sat in it when he moved out of the way.

"That Ben is a character," her father murmured with a shake of his head.

"Mmmm." Abbie made an agreeing sound as she took a sip of coffee from her cup. Her gaze wandered idly over the crowd of people and stopped when it found Seth Talbot. She felt again that quiver of purely sexual reaction to his rough good looks.

"Penny for your thoughts?" Her father tipped his head curiously at her. "Who are you staring at?"

"Our new pastor," she admitted, and this time managed to keep her poise. "Have you met him yet?"

"No. Which one is he?" He turned to survey the crowd.

"That tall man over there, talking to Mrs. Smith." Abbie pointed him out with one finger, not wanting to be too obvious.

"Him?" There was vague surprise. "He doesn't look like a minister."

Laughter bubbled in her throat. "That's what I said, too," she admitted. "Unfortunately, I was talking to him at the time."

"That isn't like you," he said, smiling along with her. "You're usually more tactful."

"Everyone's entitled to stick their foot in their mouth once in a while." Abbie shrugged. "Besides, he's the motorist I told you about—the one who patched up Mabel so I could make it into town. He drives a sports car. And he was dressed in cutoffs and a T-shirt. Believe me, he didn't look like a minister then, either."

"No wonder you were surprised," he agreed, and turned his attention back to the more immediate subject of their conversation. "What does his wife look like?"

"He's a bachelor." Abbie pretended not to hear the soft whistle of surprise from her father as she took another sip of coffee. But it was difficult to ignore him when he turned a speculating look on her.

"Do I detect a note of interest?" he asked.

"Daddy, I just met him," she protested.

"So?" he challenged.

"So, I hardly know him. Besides, he's a minister," she reasoned.

"A minister—not a priest," he reminded her.

The conversation was taking an uncomfortable turn. Abbie was glad when she saw Ben Cooper sliding through the crowd with a cup of coffee and a napkinful of tea cakes and sandwiches. She quickly rose from the chair next to her father.

"You can have your seat back, Ben," she declared brightly, and pretended to eye the blueberry tart balanced on top of the small sandwiches. "I think I'll check out the sweets."

One blueberry tart and a cup of coffee later, Abbie found herself trapped in a conversation with the Coltrain sisters, two delightful ladies in their eighties who could ramble on for hours, reminiscing about the past. She'd heard nearly all their stories at least twice. It was inevitable that her attention wandered.

She seemed to have only one interest—Seth Talbot. Voluntarily or involuntarily, she had spent most of her time observing the way he casually mingled, getting acquainted with the members of his new congregation attending the tea. It wasn't just the women who seemed to take to him, but the men as well. The room seemed to buzz with conversations with the new minister as their main topic.

It might have been a farewell tea for Reverend Augustus, but Seth Talbot was stealing the man's thunder. Or was it only her imagination? Just because she was practically obsessed with him did not necessarily mean that everyone else was. Abbie sighed, pulling her attention back to the moment as she took a drink of coffee and discovered it had grown cold.

"Would you?" Isabel Coltrain turned an unblinking pair of blue eyes to Abbie.

"I . . ." She realized she hadn't heard a word of the recent conversation. "I'm sorry." Abbie pretended there were too many other people talking. "What did you say?"

"Would you type the manuscript Esther and I are writing when we're finished?" The older of the two sisters repeated the question. "We'll pay you . . . if it's not too much."

"Yes, I'd be happy to type it for you." Abbie relaxed a little, now that she knew exactly what she was committing herself to do. "I can do it in the evenings."

"I'm so glad that young man suggested that we should write a book, aren't you, Esther?" Isabel Coltrain practically sparkled with zest and energy.

"Young man?" Abbie murmured in vague confusion. She had been under the impression that the manuscript was already in progress.

"Yes, the new reverend." Esther showed equal excitement. "He was so fascinated by some of the stories we told him that he said we should write them down."

"My, but he's a handsome man, isn't he?" Isabel rolled her eyes and clutched a hand to her heart. "He makes me wish I was young again."

"Act your age," her younger sister scolded.

From past experience, Abbie knew the pair could become quite spiteful with sibling jealousy and quickly intervened. "It's a wonderful idea about the book. When do you plan to start on it?"

"Oh, right away," Esther assured her. "We're going to start by jotting down our ideas, then decide who's going to write what."

"That sounds practical," Abbie agreed, even though it could be the basis for a lot of arguments. Before she became embroiled in the middle of one, she thought it best to excuse herself. "I think I'll warm up my coffee."

"Don't drink too much. It isn't good for you," Isabel warned.

"I won't," Abbie promised while she backed away.

Chapter Three

The old Roman-numeraled clock on the office wall indicated the time was five minutes before twelve noon. Abbie opened the bottom drawer of her desk and removed her purse, a large shoulder-bag affair. Lifting the flap, she took a slightly oversized compact mirror out of a side compartment and a tube of bronzed pink lipstick.

The overhead light didn't provide the best conditions for the application of makeup but it was infinitely better than the bare light bulb in the rest room. Abbie turned in her swivel chair so she was facing the full play of light while she freshened the color of her lips and inspected the results in the mirror. She used her fingertips to fluff the ends of her copper hair, then snapped the compact mirror closed in satisfaction.

She was just replacing it in its zippered compartment in her purse when her father stepped out of his private office. His suit jacket was off and the sleeves of his white shirt were rolled back. He had a cup in his hand. It didn't require any clever deduction for Abbie to figure out he was heading to the coffee urn for more coffee. He'd been up to his elbows in law books for the last hour. Case research always seemed to go hand in hand with increased coffee consumption.

His absentminded glance at her desk took in her purse sitting atop it, which seemed to prompt a look at the antique wall clock. "It's that time already, is it?" He sighed his disbelief that the morning could have gone so quickly and walked on, then stopped. "Don't forget to make that bank deposit."

"I've got it right here." Abbie picked up the envelope from her desk top. "I plan to stop at the bank first. Are you going out for lunch, or would you like me to bring you something?"

Her father paused in the act of filling his cup to send her a frowning look. "Is Ed coming in at one or one-thirty?"

Abbie checked the appointment book. "One."

"Better bring me a sandwich then," he decided.

Standing up, Abbie slipped the long strap to her purse over her shoulder and kept the envelope with the bank deposit in her hand. "I'll be back in an hour or soooner," she said, and received an acknowledging nod from her father.

With a hot sun overhead, Abbie kept to the shady side of the street. There was a good breeze, which kept the summer heat from becoming stifling. It billowed the ice-blue material

50

of her loose, tentlike dress, cinched at the waist with a wide white elastic belt.

The streets and sidewalks were bustling with summer traffic as Abbie walked to the bank. There were so many strangers about that she stopped looking for familiar faces. When she reached to open the door to the bank, a man's hand was there ahead of her. She half turned to absently smile a polite thanks for the gentlemanly gesture. But the man leaning forward was Seth Talbot, not a stranger.

The air seemed to leave her lungs in a sudden rush. Abbie wasn't prepared for this exposure to his virile brand of sexuality. For the last three days, she'd made a determined attempt to block him out of her mind and stop weaving romantic fantasies about a minister of the church.

"How are you today, Miss Scott?" Seth greeted her with a natural friendly warmth.

It took a tremendous force of will to pull her gaze from his roughly hewn features and the arresting indigo of his eyes, but Abbie succeeded in doing so. "Fine, thank you, Reverend." She was irritated by how prim she sounded and made a stilted attempt to correct it. "And you?"

There was a hint of amusement in his gaze when Abbie dared to glance at him again. "Very well." But there was nothing in his voice to mock her as he held the door to the bank open, then followed her inside.

Her stomach felt like a quivering ball of nerves. The summer season had brought its usual mixture of sightseers and customers to the bank. Its reconstruction as a Victorian-era institution made it one of the town's attractions.

Believing the conversation was over, Abbie skirted the high-backed chairs that were arranged around a polished potbellied stove, a brass cuspidor near one foot, and headed for the brass teller cages. Then she realized he was walking beside her. Again he was dressed in an unorthodox fashion for a minister—a pair of Levi's that hugged his narrow hips and long, muscular legs, and a white sport shirt that was unbuttoned at the throat. His shoes looked suspiciously like cowboy boots.

It was one thing for him to travel in casual clothes, but Abbie was astounded that he was going around town minus his frock and white collar. This was the community he was to serve as minister, but how would anyone know it when he dressed like everyone else?

His gaze had finished its sweep of the bank's unusual interior and stopped on her. "It really carries out the town's theme, doesn't it?" he remarked.

"Yes. They have quite a display of original business machines, too," Abbie replied, feeling the tension return with the attention he was paying her.

"I looked at them when I was in here Monday." He nodded, his burnished gold hair reflecting the light from the overhead chandeliers. "Are you downtown shopping or is this your lunch break?"

The personal query caught her off guard. "My

lunch break," Abbie admitted, then felt she needed an excuse for being in the bank. She nervously lifted the hand with the envelope. "I have a deposit to make first, though."

"Where do you work?" His question appeared to contain only idle interest.

"I'm a legal secretary—for my father." It was hardly a secret.

"There's nothing like nepotism to keep out of the unemployment lines," he declared with the flash of a white smile.

Abbie stiffened, taking offense even though she knew none had been intended. "I happen to be very qualified for the job."

An eyebrow was arched briefly, his look gentling at her sensitivity. "I'm not throwing stones, Miss Scott. After all, I work for my Father." A teasing light sparkled in his blue eyes and Abbie smiled at the comparison of their respective employers. "That's better." Seth smiled too. "Would you excuse me? I have to talk to one of the officers."

"Of course." She hadn't meant to keep him from his errand, and her smile slid away. "I need to make this deposit, too." It was a defensive reply, an insistence that she had things to do as well.

The nearest teller also happened to be the one with the shortest waiting line. Abbie walked to it, aware of Seth Talbot approaching the desk of a bank officer. The two customers ahead of her had only minor transactions to make, so it was quickly Abbie's turn at the window.

"Hello, Roberta," Abbie greeted the plump, young woman teller, and slid the deposit across the counter.

"Is it as hot outside as it looks?" the teller asked as she checked to verify that there were signatures and deposit-only stamps on all the checks.

"Hotter, but there's a nice breeze," Abbie replied.

A bleached blonde crowded close to Roberta and leaned toward Abbie to whisper eagerly. "We're all just dying to find out who that gorgeous hunk of man is that you're with?" Fran was a former classmate of Abbie's, who was married and had two children, but she'd always been a little man-crazy.

"What man?" As soon as Abbie asked she realized Fran was talking about Seth—Reverend Talbot.

"What man she says." Fran gave Roberta a knowing look.

"I guess you're referring to Reverend Talbot," Abbie admitted. "He's the new pastor of our church now that Reverend Augustus has retired."

"That is the new pastor!" Fran's stage whisper seemed alarmingly loud. "Oh, Roberta, I think I've just been saved," she declared on a giggle.

"I don't blame you," Roberta murmured, and cast a longing eye across the bank—no doubt at Seth, but Abbie refused to turn around and look. "He's the sexiest-looking man to come to this town in a long time."

"I guess," Fran agreed effusively. "I'm going to have to buy myself a new Sunday dress to wear to church."

"Do you belong to our church?" Abbie questioned with a blank look. She couldn't recall ever seeing Fran and her husband attend Sunday services.

"I haven't been there in years—not since Butch and I got married," Fran admitted indifferently, then grinned coyly. "But I think I'm going to be among the faithful from now on."

"Heck, I think I'm going to convert." Roberta smiled impishly.

"Oh, God," Fran murmured excitedly. "He's coming over here. Oh, Abbie, you've just got to introduce us."

She was disgusted at the way the two of them were carrying on about him. One glance at the other female employees behind the cages informed her that Roberta and Fran weren't the only ones avidly eyeing the man walking up, and whispering among themselves. They were only echoing her own reaction to him, but that didn't make it any less distasteful.

Roberta passed Abbie the receipt for her deposit and spoke loudly, "Here you are, Abbie."

"Thank you." She was holding her neck almost rigidly still to avoid turning her head to look at Seth Talbot when he stopped beside her. But she had to move to put the receipt in her purse.

"Are you finished?" he asked.

"Yes." Her glance bounced away before it

squarely met his eyes. Too many sensations were clawing at her because of his presence.

"Hi, I'm Fran Bigsby." The blonde introduced herself when Abbie failed to do it immediately. "Abbie was just telling us that you're the new pastor. Welcome to Eureka Springs."

"Seth Talbot's the name and I'm glad to be here." Again, that warm smiling look was on his visage.

"I'm Roberta Flack, no relation to the singer." Roberta beamed, looking very pretty, despite the unflattering pounds she carried.

"I'm happy to meet you both," he said. When Abbie started to move away from the teller's window so Roberta could wait on the next customer, Seth started to leave with her. "Maybe I'll see you in church some Sunday," he added as a farewell remark.

"You can be sure of it," Fran called after them.

Abbie couldn't walk away from the window fast enough, embarrassed without being sure why. But Seth was undeterred by her haste, easily striding at her side.

"Was there anyplace special you were going to have lunch?" he asked.

His query startled a glance from her. "No. Why?" There were others leaving the bank, and Abbie was forced to slow her pace as she scanned his expression.

"I was on my way to lunch. You're on your way to lunch. So why don't we have it together?" Seth reasoned smoothly. "There's a restaurant just down the street. Shall we go there?"

Her acceptance of his plan seemed to be taken for granted. Actually, Abbie couldn't think of a single reason why she should refuse. "Sounds good," she agreed.

The combination of noon hour and the influx of summer visitors resulted in a crowded restaurant. Luckily, Abbie and Seth had to wait only a few minutes before they were seated at a small table, hardly big enough for two. Her knees kept bumping against his under the table no matter how she tried to angle them in the close quarters. There was another man seated in a chair directly behind her, so she couldn't even edge her chair away from the table.

"Sorry," she apologized when her knee rubbed against the side of his for the fourth time. She hoped he didn't think she was doing it deliberately.

"It's close quarters in here." Seth offered the excuse, but the light glinting in his blue eyes made her feel hot.

"Yes, it is." Abbie opened her menu to study it intently. Maybe if she sat perfectly still and didn't move, it wouldn't be so bad.

"What are you going to have?" he asked as he spread open his menu.

"A chef's salad, I think." Her stomach wasn't behaving too well. She didn't want to put a lot of food into it. "How about you?"

But when she looked up, his gaze was making a leisurely survey of her upper body and appearing to take particular note of the hint of maturely rounded breasts under the loose-fitting dress. It was the look of a man, and a hundred alarm bells rang in her ears.

"Are you on a diet?" Seth finally lifted his gaze to her face. "It's just one man's opinion, but I don't see how you can improve on your figure."

In the first place, she wasn't sure if he should notice such things, and she definitely felt he shouldn't comment on them if he did. But how on earth did you reprimand a minister? Abbie preferred to believe she had misinterpreted his glance. Maybe it had been more analytical and less intimate.

"I don't like to eat a lot of food on a hot day like today." She chose to explain away her lack of appetite.

"That's probably very wise," he agreed. When the waitress came, Seth ordered for both of them. At the last minute, Abbie remembered she had promised to bring her father a sandwich.

"I'll need a cold roast-beef sandwich to go, too, please," she added hastily, then explained to Seth when the waitress left, "My father was tied up and couldn't get away for lunch."

"He's an attorney here?"

"Yes. It's just a small practice. He keeps talking about retiring but he won't. He loves what he's doing too much." It seemed easier to talk about her father than the other choice of subjects open to her—like the weather. "Although he does complain that his practice interferes with his fishing," she added with a laughing smile.

"He's an avid fisherman, I take it." Seth smiled.

"Very avid," Abbie agreed, and couldn't help thinking that Seth was a "Fisher of Men."

"I didn't have a chance to meet him last Sunday at the tea. I'm looking forward to it, though," he said. "How long have you worked for him?"

"About a year now." Abbie leaned back in her chair when the waitress returned to set a glass of iced tea in front of her and milk for Seth. The action accidentally pressed more of her leg against his.

"Don't worry," he murmured on a seductively low-pitched note. "I'm not going to think you're playing footsy with me under the table." Abbie was positive she had never blushed in her life, but her cheeks were on fire at the moment. Her mind was absolutely blank of anything to say. Seth seemed to guess and asked, "What did you do before that? Attend college?"

"No, I worked for TWA in Kansas City." She was relieved to have the subject changed.

"As a stewardess?"

"No, I was in management, in the corporate offices."

His attention deepened. Abbie braced herself for the next question, fully anticipating that he was going to ask why she had left, but it never came. There was only the quiet study of his keen eyes.

"Thomas Wolfe was obviously wrong. It is

possible to go home again," was the only comment he made.

"I'm just a small-town girl at heart," she admitted.

Just as the waitress came with their luncheon order, a local judge paused by their table. Abbie had known Judge Sessions since she was a small child, so she wasn't surprised by his greeting when he noticed her.

"Hi there, little girl. How are you doing today?" He grabbed a lock of copper hair and tugged at it affectionately.

"I'm doing just fine, Judge." She smiled up at him.

His glance went to Seth, sitting opposite from her. "Who's this with you? A new man friend?" His teasing demand was accompanied by a broad wink.

"No, of course not." Abbie denied this quickly, conscious that Seth was already rising to be introduced. "This is the new minister of our church, Reverend Seth Talbot. Reverend, I'd like you to meet Judge Sessions, a family friend."

"Reverend?" The judge almost did a double take, then shook Seth's hand and laughed. "You could have fooled me!"

"I seem to fool a lot of people," Seth admitted with a brief glance at Abbie.

"You do look more like a man of the flesh than a man of the cloth," the judge stated.

"I'm the usual combination of both," Seth replied, not at all bothered by the remark.

Abbie thought the judge's description was very accurate. Seth was made of flesh and blood, all hard, male sinew and bone. Not even the cloth could conceal that.

"I'm glad to hear it." The judge nodded. "We need a change from sanctimonious old fogies, too old to sin anymore." He laid a hand on Abbie's shoulder. "Be nice to this little girl here. They don't come any better than Abbie." Then he was moving away from their table with a farewell wave of his hand.

This time it was Seth who brushed his knee against hers when he sat down. Abbie wondered if she wouldn't feel more relaxed if it weren't for this constant physical contact with him. Her skirt had inched up above her knees, but it was impossible to pull it down without touching him. He couldn't see it, not with the table in the way, so she made no attempt to adjust it downward.

"Have you known the judge long?" Seth asked as he picked up his silverware to begin eating his chicken-fried steak with gravy smothered over it and the mound of mashed potatoes.

"Practically all my life." She stabbed a piece of lettuce and sliced ham with her fork. "It's not surprising that people are taken aback when they find out you're a minister. You really should wear your collar, so they'll at least have some advance warning."

If he'd been wearing it, the judge wouldn't have assumed he was her boyfriend, and the girls at the bank wouldn't have been lusting over him—and maybe she would feel a little safer.

The last seemed silly, yet Abbie felt the collar would provide some sort of protection for her.

"Do you have any idea how those stiff collars chafe your neck on a hot day like this?" Seth appeared amused by her comment.

"I'm sorry. I didn't mean to criticize the way you're dressed." It had been a very rude thing to do—as well as presumptuous.

"It doesn't matter." His wide shoulders were lifted in a careless shrug. There was a dancing light in his eyes when he looked at her. "I promise you that I do wear it when I make my rounds at the hospital or call on a member of the congregation in their home."

"In some ways, this is a very conservative community. I guess that's what I'm trying to say," Abbie murmured. And he seemed liberal and at the age to know about sin, as the judge had suggested.

"Right in the heart of the Bible Belt area, I know." He nodded.

She glanced at him sharply to see if there was any mockery in his expression, but it was impossible to tell. Her gaze wandered downward to the white of his shirt. With the top three buttons unfastened, she had a glimpse of curly gold chest hairs, another example of his blatant masculinity. There was a chain of some sort around his neck, too.

"Something wrong?" Seth caught her staring, and amusement deepened the edges of his mouth without materializing into a smile.

Her pulse did a quick acceleration as Abbie

dived her fork into the salad again. "You just don't look like a minister." She sighed the admission. His latent sensuality was too unnerving for her.

His low chuckle vibrated over her tingling nerve ends. "Let's see . . . what would laymen expect a minister to look like?" he mused. "I imagine there are different categories. The intensely pious should be pale, ascetically slender, with deep-set eyes, hollow cheeks, and a fervid voice. There'd be the benevolent father figure— white hair, a round face, and a kindly air. And you have the thunderer, preaching about the wrath of God and pointing out the sinners with a long accusing finger. He'd have a beard, be very tall, with beetle brows." Seth paused to send a mocking glance across the table. "How am I doing so far?"

"I guess I've been guilty of type-casting," Abbie admitted with a faint smile.

"Everyone does it," he assured her. "Now, my idea of a legal secretary is a woman in her forties with her hair pulled back in a severe bun. She'd wear wire-rimmed glasses and tailored business suits." His glance skimmed her again. "Funny, you don't look like a legal secretary."

She laughed naturally for the first time. "I promise I won't say it again, Reverend." Inside, Abbie knew she'd think it each time she referred to him by his professional title.

"I've finally made you laugh." His gaze focused on the parted curve of her lips. She felt them tremble from the look that was oddly physical. "We've cleared the first hurdle," Seth murmured enigmatically.

"To what?" Her voice sounded breathless.

"To becoming friends," he replied.

"Oh." For some reason, Abbie was disappointed by his answer. She ate a few more mouthfuls of salad but found it tasteless. She couldn't stop being conscious of the warmth of his leg against hers, and the rough texture of the denim material brushing the bareness of her calf. It became imperative to keep a conversation going. "Are you all moved in to the parsonage?"

"More or less. I still have a lot of boxes of books to unpack." There was a rueful slant to his mouth as he glanced at her. "Have you ever been in it?"

"No." The slight shake of her head swayed the ends of her pale copper hair.

"It's a rambling monstrosity. There's more rooms there than I'll ever use. I'll probably close up half of the house."

"I imagine it was intended for a family to live in rather than a single man," Abbie suggested.

"It's practically an unwritten rule. A man is supposed to have his wife picked out *before* he graduates from the seminary and is assigned to his first church." Seth didn't appear troubled that he hadn't followed the rule.

"But you didn't." She stated the obvious.

"No, I didn't," he agreed, and let his gaze lock on to hers.

Her throat muscles tightened. "I guess it is the expected thing—for a minister to be married, I mean," Abbie finally managed to get the words out. "How long have you been in the ministry?" She guessed his age to be somewhere in the range of thirty-five.

"Thirteen years. I spent four of those years as an air-force chaplain." He dropped his gaze and began slicing off a piece of steak.

"Where was your first church?" She gave in to her curiosity and began delving into his background.

"This is my first church," he admitted.

"You mean, you were always an assistant pastor before?" A slight frown of confusion creased her forehead.

"No. I worked in the national offices of the church. My work was more business-oriented than anything else." There was a sardonic curve to his mouth. "For a variety of reasons, I requested to be assigned a church in some quiet little community. I guess I'm taking something like a sabbatical."

"I see," she murmured.

"I doubt it." He showed a bit of cynical skepticism, then hid it. "But it isn't important." His glance suddenly challenged her. "Why is it that *you* aren't married, Miss Scott?"

Her mouth opened and closed twice before she could think of a safe answer. She laughed shortly to conceal her hesitation. "Grandmother Klein says it's because I haven't looked hard enough."

"Or maybe you've been looking in all the wrong places," Seth suggested.

It was on the tip of her tongue to ask him where the right places were, but Abbie resisted the impulse. "Maybe," she conceded, and stirred the half-eaten salad with her fork. Absently she glanced at the slim, gold watch around her wrist. Her eyes widened when she saw the time. "It's after one. I have to get back to the office." She laid her napkin alongside the salad plate and reached for the luncheon check the waitress had left, but Seth was quicker. Her hand ended up tangling briefly with his fingers, the contact sending a tingling shock up her arm.

"I'll buy this time," he insisted.

"Please," Abbie protested. "I don't really have time to argue. She opened her purse to take out her money, intending to leave it on the table regardless of what he said.

"You said yourself that you're short on time," Seth reminded her. "If you insist on paying, just put whatever you feel you owe in the collection plate this Sunday."

"I . . . all right." She gave in to his persuasion and refastened the leather flap of her purse.

"Don't forget your father's sandwich." He handed her the paper sack when she started to get up without it.

"Thank you." She gratefully took it from him. It was bad enough being late without her father having to go hungry, too.

"See you Sunday."

The walk to her father's office seemed longer

than it was. Abbie suspected it was because she was late and trying to hurry so she wouldn't be later than she was already. Her father was a tolerant, easygoing man, but he was a stickler for punctuality.

When she walked in, the door to his private office was closed, but she could hear muffled conversation within. His one o'clock appointment had obviously arrived. Abbie hurried to her desk, returning her purse to the lower drawer and setting his sandwich atop her desk. She swiveled her chair to the typewriter and picked up the headset to the dictaphone. Before she had it comfortably adjusted so she could hear, his door opened.

Abbie saw his irritation as he approached her desk. "I left a file on your desk." He picked up a folder from the IN tray.

"Here's your sandwich." She handed him the sack.

"I'm surprised you remembered. What kept you?"

"I had lunch with Reverend Talbot." She knew the judge would mention it if she didn't. Besides, keeping it a secret would only mean there was something to hide. "The time just slipped away."

He harumphed but didn't comment. Instead he opened the sack to peer inside. "Roast beef?"

"Yes."

There was a relenting of his stern expression. "At least you brought back my favorite."

Chapter Four

There were more people at church than Abbie remembered seeing in a long time, especially since it wasn't Easter or Christmas. A lot of it, she guessed, was curiosity about the new minister. Seth made a striking figure standing at the pulpit in his robe while he conducted the services.

He was halfway through his sermon before Abbie realized he wasn't using a microphone, yet his well-modulated voice carried his words effortlessly to the back row. He talked easily, as if he was carrying on a conversation instead of giving a sermon. His gestures were natural rather than dramatic. There were even places where the congregation laughed at a bit of humor that contained a message.

It seemed that Seth had barely begun when he finished. Abbie would have liked him to go on, and it was the first time she could ever remember wishing a sermon had been longer. She stole a glance at her parents sitting in the pew beside her. Her father was looking at his watch with a stunned expression, while her mother continued to give her rapt attention to the man at the pulpit.

A few minutes later, they were following the people filing out of church. The line moved slowly as those ahead of them paused to shake hands with the minister on their way out the door.

Her father leaned sideways to murmur, "Your reverend isn't bad, Abbie."

"He's not *my* reverend, Dad," she corrected in an equally low voice, not liking the insinuation that she was somehow linked to Seth simply because she'd had lunch with him once.

"If you say so." He shrugged, letting her move ahead of him as it became a single-file line to greet Seth.

Abbie waited patiently for her turn, a ripple of anticipation warming her blood while she watched Seth chatting with the couple ahead of her. The black robe seemed to make his hair look darker, more brown than gold, but the trappings of the clergy didn't alter his male appeal.

His glance strayed to her and lingered briefly in recognition. The vivid blue of his eyes darkened with a glow that made her feel special. The look tripped her heartbeat but Abbie refused to flatter herself into believing it held any significance. She was just a familiar face, someone he knew after meeting so many strangers.

The exchange of glances lasted only a few seconds before his attention reverted to the couple. Then they were moving down the steps and it was Abbie's turn. Close up, Seth seemed taller, more commanding in his black robe. His hand reached to take hers in greeting and continued to hold it when Abbie would have withdrawn it.

"What's the verdict?" There was warm, mocking amusement in the downward glance that took in his preaching robes. "Will I pass?" He was teasing her about the way she had criticized him about his dress at lunch that day.

"Yes." The corners of her mouth dimpled with a responding smile. "And you *sounded* like a minister, too, Reverend."

His head was tipped back to release a throaty laugh. Its volume was subdued, but no less genuine. Seth inclined his head to her in mocking acknowledgment. "That's the highest compliment I've received today. I thank you, Miss Scott."

"You're welcome, Reverend." She would have moved on, but his firm grip wouldn't relinquish her hand. There was uncertain confusion in the look she gave him, but his attention had swerved to her parents.

"Is this your father?" Seth inquired in a tone that prompted her to make the introduction.

"Yes. I'd like you to meet him." Only when she spoke to indicate her compliance with his unspoken request did Seth release her hand. "Dad, this is Reverend Talbot. Reverend, my father, Drew Scott. You've met my mother already."

"Yes, I have." He nodded, shaking her hand.

"It's good to see you again, Mrs. Scott. And it's a pleasure to meet your husband. How do you do, Mr. Scott."

"I've been looking forward to meeting you, Reverend," her father admitted. "Enjoyed your sermon."

"I understand you're a fisherman." Seth didn't mention that Abbie had been the source of that information, but her father guessed it. "Maybe you can point me to some good fishing holes around here later on."

"Be happy to," her father agreed, then added a qualification, "as long as you make sure the next time you take my secretary out to lunch, she's not late getting back."

"Daddy." It was a low, impatient protest Abbie made. He made it sound like she was likely to have lunch with Seth again.

But Seth wasn't bothered by the implication. "You have a deal, Mr. Scott."

There were still more people behind them waiting to leave the church. Abbie was relieved when her parents moved past Seth to descend the steps with her. Not all the congregation had dispersed once they left the church. Some were scattered along the wide sidewalk, socializing in small groups. Her parents were too well known to go directly to their car without being stopped by someone. Since Abbie had ridden with them, she was obliged to linger on the fringes each time her father or mother paused to speak to someone.

Her glance invariably wandered back to the

church doors. She recognized Fran Bigsby when she came out with her two small children. There was no sign of her husband as the bleached blonde stopped to talk to Seth. Flirt with him seemed a better description, Abbie thought cattily. There was no sign of Fran's husband but she noticed her younger sister, Marjorie, was with her.

Suddenly, Abbie realized there were a lot of women that had attended the morning service without their husbands, especially those families who weren't regular worshipers. She didn't like the conclusion she was reaching because she had the unkind suspicion they hadn't been drawn there today to welcome their new minister, but rather to meet the handsome bachelor-pastor the whole town was buzzing about.

It made her silent, and more than just a little thoughtful, while she studied her own motives. No matter how she tried, Abbie couldn't ignore the fact that she was strongly attracted to him on a physical level. She was living in a glass house and couldn't very well afford to throw stones at anyone else.

Abbie glanced at the clock as she rolled the finished letter out of the typewriter. It was close to noon, time enough to type an envelope and have the letter ready to mail before she left for lunch. It was Thursday, exactly a week to the day since she'd lunched with Seth.

The knowledge must have been hovering at the back of her mind, because when she heard

72

the street door open, her heart did a little somersault. She turned, expecting to see Seth walking into the office. But Judge Sessions didn't look like him at all. It was difficult to keep her smile from dying.

"Hello, Judge." Abbie forced the cheerfulness into her voice. "Dad's in his office. You can go in, if you want. He doesn't have a client with him."

"Maybe I didn't come to see him," he challenged lightly. "Maybe I'm here to see you."

"It's possible, but I doubt it." Now that she had gotten over her initial disappointment, Abbie could respond more naturally to the judge's teasing remarks.

Her father stepped out of his private office. "I thought I heard you out here, Walter," he accused, and crossed to exchange a back slapping handshake. "What are you doing, you old crook?"

"I came to take my favorite father-daughter pair to lunch," the judge replied, then slid Abbie a glittering look. "That is, if your daughter doesn't have a previous luncheon date?"

"I believe I have a vacancy in my social calendar today," she replied, laughing.

"You could have been saving all your free time for that handsome new reverend," the judge suggested. "When are you going to see him again?"

Abbie was beginning to lose her humor at his probing remarks. "Probably Sunday at church just like everyone else," she retorted with a trace of coolness. "Just because I had lunch with him once, purely by accident, it doesn't mean it's going to become a regular event."

"Drew, I think the girl's sick," the judge declared. "She's trying to claim she's not interested in this fellow."

"I'm not," Abbie protested, and wanted to bite her tongue for telling such an outright lie.

"What makes you different from all the rest of the women in town?" He challenged her with a disbelieving look. "From what I've heard, they're falling all over themselves trying to get his attention."

"Is that a fact?" her father inserted, siding with the judge to gang up on Abbie. "All the gossip manages to get funneled to you, Walter. Why don't you let us in on it?"

"I understand that his cup runneth over. The older ladies are bringing him casseroles, cakes, salads, cookies, homemade bread, and just about anything else you care to mention. There isn't a bare shelf in his refrigerator or cupboard."

"I think that's nice," Abbie insisted in defense of the gifts. "It's the neighborly thing to do when a newcomer moves in."

"But those old ladies are wise." The judge winked slyly. "The way to a man's heart is through his stomach. Haven't you heard?"

"Come to think of it, Alice baked him a green-apple pie just this last Tuesday," Drew recalled. "Maybe I'd better keep a closer eye on my wife. She was at the parsonage for almost an hour."

"Dad, you can't be jealous of the reverend."

Abbie wasn't sure if he was serious or just razzing her.

"I don't mind if she looks . . . as long as that's all she does," he said, then laughed to show he wasn't worried.

"It seems there are a lot of young wives who have suddenly discovered they have marital problems, which came as quite a surprise to their contented husbands . . ." the judge inserted. ". . . and now they're going to the good reverend for his advice and understanding."

Abbie had the uneasy feeling that Fran Bigsby was probably one of them. She saw the point the judge was making. It was all a ruse to get Seth's undivided attention, to try to attract his interest.

"But it's more than his sympathy they're after," her father added, confirming Abbie's private thoughts.

"Women are volunteering right and left to help with anything from typing the church bulletins to doing his housekeeping." The judge gave an exaggerated sigh and looked at her father. "And they say a bachelor's life is a lonely one. One crook of his little finger and half the women in the county would come running. I'll bet the church will be filled to the rafters next Sunday."

"I wouldn't be surprised," her father agreed with this summation.

That's when Abbie made the decision that she wouldn't be one of them. She didn't want Seth to get the impression she was chasing him just like all the other women in town seemed to be. She didn't necessarily attend church every single

Sunday, so it wouldn't be out of the ordinary for her to skip a couple of weeks.

She was very casual about it when she talked to her mother on Saturday and mentioned that she was going to visit Grandmother Klein on Sunday and skip church. Her mother took Abbie's decision at face value. Her father gave her a strange look but said nothing.

On Monday morning, Abbie didn't have a chance to make the first pot of coffee before the street door opened and the two Coltrain sisters came bustling in. They always seemed to wear outfits that clashed with what the other one was wearing. Esther had on a brightly flowered dress, predominantly grape-colored, while Isabel wore a gaudy, fushia-pink dress.

"There you are, Abbie!" Esther declared happily. The fluorescent lights in the office seemed to reflect the grape from her dress and cast a lavender tint on her curling white hair. "We thought we might find you here at your papa's office."

"Yes, I work here during the week," Abbie explained, certain she had told them that before.

But neither of them had ever worked. They had been raised to believe women should stay in the home, married or not. Luckily the inheritance from their parents had left them with substantial annuities so they could.

Isabel opened her enormous black tapestry bag with its bold pink-rose design, and pulled out a stack of loose papers in assorted sizes and colors. A slim rubber band strained to hold them together.

"We were going to give you this yesterday at church but you didn't come," Isabel explained.

"What is it?" Abbie reached for it with a puzzled frown.

"Don't you remember?" Esther looked stricken. "You said you'd type our manuscript for us."

"Do you mean you've written it already?" Abbie looked up from the first piece of paper, filled with scrawly handwriting, to stare incredulously at the two sisters.

"Oh, goodness no!" Isabel laughed merrily at the thought. "We decided it would be easier if we gave you what we had finished as we went along."

"Haven't we gotten a lot done?" Esther asked excitedly. "We worked on it every single day, didn't we, Isabel?"

"It was so much fun, Abbie," Isabel declared, puffing up with proud satisfaction. "I'm so glad the reverend suggested it."

"I can imagine." Abbie couldn't recall when she had seen either sister so animated or so enthused. It was contagious. She felt herself catching their excitement too, and smiling right along with them.

"I do hope you won't have any trouble reading it." Isabel cupped a hand to her mouth to whisper secretively to Abbie. "Esther used to have such beautiful penmanship, but with her arthritis it's sometimes not very legible."

"I don't think I'll have any difficulty. But if I have any questions on a particular part, I'll call and ask," she promised.

"We aren't telling anyone what we're doing." Esther put a protective hand over the uncompleted manuscript Abbie was holding. "You're the only one who knows."

"I won't breathe a word." Abbie crossed her heart in a child's solemn promise. "In fact, I'll put it in the bottom drawer of my desk right now."

"You won't lose it." Isabel looked worried as Abbie walked to her desk to put the handwritten papers away.

"Call us as soon as you have it typed," Esther advised. "We'll have some more ready for you." She took her sister's arm. "Come, Isabel. Let's go home so we can start on the next part."

"Bye!" Abbie called as the two white-haired sisters bustled toward the door. "I'll phone you when I'm through with this."

That evening was the start of what became a nightly routine, with her portable typewriter sitting on the small dining-room table in her apartment and the pages of the manuscript setting out. The Coltrain sisters had used everything from yellow tablet paper to fancy stationery to write on. Abbie quickly discovered that the page numbers on the sheets were not necessarily correct. More often than not, they were out of sequence.

Before she could start typing, she had to decipher the handwriting and read and arrange the pages in their proper order. She had expected the manuscript to be a collection of loosely connected anecdotes of their early years and stories of some of the area's first citizens. Abbie was shocked to realize the sisters had fictionalized it into a story—a rather torrid, period romance set in Eureka Springs around the turn of the century.

Each night, Abbie sat down to the typewriter for three hours, correcting misspelled words, or finding the right one when a sister had fallen victim to malapropism, and inserting the right punctuation where none existed. It was a long, tedious process, made fascinating by the characters and stories she remembered the sisters telling as they became part of the plot. Just when she became used to reading Esther's handwriting and could get some typing speed, the next part would be written by Isabel and she'd have to slow down again.

The typing gave her a perfect excuse to miss church that Sunday, and the sisters had more written when Abbie finished the first installment. She missed the following Sunday's service as well.

The long days, working at the office and in her apartment on the nights and weekends, were beginning to wear on her. Abbie was dragging Monday morning when she arrived at the office. She was leaning on the table, waiting for the coffee to finish dripping. Her father walked out of his office, carrying his cup, just as she was in the middle of a large yawn.

"You can't keep this up, Abbie." He shook his head at her. "You need to get out and have some fun. I hear you hammering away at that typewriter every night."

"I'll take tonight off, Dad," Abbie promised, and tried to swallow another yawn.

"Not just tonight," he advised. "You take a couple or three nights off. Go to a movie—or ask some guy for a date. These are liberated times. You don't have to wait for a Sadie Hawkins' Day."

"Yes, Dad." She smiled wryly, because there wasn't anyone she was interested in asking— except Seth. She shook away that thought. The red light blinked on to indicate the coffee was done. "Coffee's ready."

"I've just got time for a quick cup, then I have to get over to the courthouse," he said with a quick glance at his watch.

By the time her father left, Abbie had drunk her first cup of coffee and felt that at least her eyes were open. She poured a second cup and sat down at her desk to see what dictation had been left for her to type. The more she thought about her father's suggestion, the more convinced she became that he was right. It was to the point where she was typing in her dreams.

When she heard someone enter the office, Abbie tried to summon a suitably cheerful smile to greet him. But the "him" was Seth Talbot.

Her hazel-green eyes widened in surprise, and she was suddenly very much awake.

In the past three weeks, she'd only had occasional glimpses of him behind the wheel of his dark green sports car. But here he was—in the flesh—and her pulse started fluttering crazily. As Seth approached her desk, so tall and lean and flashing her that white smile, Abbie felt weak at the knees. The whiteness of his clergyman's collar contrasted sharply with his darkly tanned neck, but her senses didn't have any respect for his attire. They were all reacting to his raw manliness, his roughly chiseled features, and deeply blue eyes.

"Hello, Reverend." Abbie was amazed that she sounded so calm.

"Good morning." His eyes crinkled at the corners, partially concealing the intensity of his scanning gaze as it swept over her. "How are you?"

"Fine." She nodded. It seemed logical to assume it was her father he came to see, so Abbie explained. "I'm sorry but my father is out of the office just now. I expect him back around noon."

"I'm not here on a legal matter." Seth corrected her thinking. "I came by to see you." He said it so casually, yet her reaction was anything but. A heady kind of excitement tingled through her nerves, while a breathlessness attacked her lungs.

"Oh?" She tipped her head to the side at an inquiring angle, her pale copper hair swinging free.

"I haven't seen you in church lately," he said. "I thought I would stop to see if there was anything wrong."

"Ah." Abbie nodded her head in bitter understanding. "The shepherd is out looking for the sheep that strayed from his flock, is that it?"

There was a slight narrowing of his gaze at the bite in her voice. "Something like that, yes," Seth admitted. "I miss having an honest critic in the congregation. If I say or do something you don't like, I know you'll tell me about it. You aren't the type to flatter my ego."

But he was flattering hers by trying to make her believe it mattered to him whether she was there or not. Except that was his job, to persuade members to attend church regularly.

"I'm sure you know how it is." Abbie shrugged. "A person goes to bed on Saturday night with the best intentions but somehow doesn't make it up in time for church the next day." The wryness in her smile was caused by many things. "I warned you I wasn't one of the truly faithful."

"And I warned you that I'd bring you back into the fold," Seth reminded her with a crooked slant to his mouth.

"So you did. Okay, I promise to be at church this Sunday. Is that good enough?" She didn't want him to do any arm twisting. If she spent too much time in his company, she was afraid he might guess that she was no different from any of the other women in town, attracted to him as a man.

"That was easy." He appeared to regard her quick capitulation with a degree of curiosity.

"'Ask and ye shall receive,'" Abbie quoted.

"That's an offer I'm not going to turn down," Seth replied as the corners of his mouth deepened in a faint smile. "Would you be willing to do some typing for me?"

"I understood you had a lot of volunteers," she countered.

"Ah, but not necessarily volunteers who can type," he explained with a mocking look. "Or maybe I should say—who can type with more than one finger."

"I'd like to help you out but I've already agreed to type a manuscript for—someone else." She kept the Coltrain sisters' authorship to herself, as they had requested. "Between doing that at nights and working here during the day, I don't have time to do any more."

"It sounds like all work and no play."

"It has been hectic," Abbie admitted, but refused to feel sorry for herself. "But I'm treating myself to a night off this evening."

"Do you have a date?"

In a small community like this, there was no point in lying. If she claimed to have a date, she'd have to produce one or be caught out. "No," she answered indifferently to show it didn't matter.

"Good. Then how about having dinner with me?" Seth invited, and leaned both hands on the front of her desk.

It was the last thing Abbie had expected. She

was so tempted to accept but—she shook her head. "Thanks but I was really planning to have a quiet evening and an early night."

"That's no problem. We'll have dinner and I'll bring you straight home so you can have a restful evening," he reasoned. "What do you like? Mexican food? Pizza? Steak?"

It was so hard to refuse. "I don't think you heard me," she said weakly.

"I'll wear my collar tonight—just for you," Seth mocked.

Abbie took a deep breath and held it a second. "You don't understand what it's like living in a small community like this, Reverend." She sighed. "If I had dinner with you tonight, by tomorrow morning, rumor would have it all over town that we're having an affair."

"So?" he challenged.

She wished he wasn't so close. Even with the desk separating them, the way he was leaning on it brought him much nearer. She could even smell the tangy fragrance of his after-shave lotion.

"*So*—you're a minister." Abbie wondered why she was reminding him. "And a bachelor. You can't afford to have that kind of talk going around."

"Empty talk can't hurt me." He hunched his shoulders in an indifferent shrug without changing his position. "It doesn't bother me, so you shouldn't let it bother you."

Abbie had run out of arguments. "It doesn't."

"Then you'll have dinner with me," Seth concluded.

"Pizza." The atmosphere at a pizza parlor would be more casual, invite less intimacy. Plus there wouldn't be any lingering after the meal. It seemed the safest choice all around.

"I'll pick you up at six-thirty. Is that all right?"

"Yes, that's fine." Abbie nodded, certain that she had lost her senses completely. "Do you know where I live?"

"Yes. Your address is in the membership files," he said, indicating he'd already checked. Deliberately or just as a matter of course, Abbie didn't know.

"It's probably my parents' address that's listed. I live in the apartment above the garage," she explained.

Seth straightened from her desk. "I lived in a garret when I was attending the seminary. My friends and I had some good times there."

"I like it," Abbie murmured in response.

"I won't keep you from your work any longer," he said. "I don't want to get into any more trouble with your father over that." But he was smiling in a way that belied his expression of concern. "I'll see you tonight."

"Yes." Abbie just hoped that she knew what she was doing.

Chapter Five

At ten after five that afternoon, Abbie was clearing her desk to leave. Her father stepped out of his office, a pair of reading glasses sitting low on his nose and a letter in his hand.

"I've changed my mind about the way I want this letter worded, Abbie. I'll need to have you retype it," he said, hardly paying any attention to what she was doing.

"You don't have to have it yet this afternoon, do you?" she asked hopefully. "It's already after five."

He bent his wrist to look at his watch. "I hadn't realized it was that late already. You don't mind staying a few more minutes while I reword this. There's no reason for you to rush home."

"As a matter of fact there is," Abbie admitted. "I have a date."

He took off his glasses to look at her. "Since when?" He was surprised. "Don't tell me you took my advice and asked a man out?"

"No." She wasn't quite *that* liberated. "Reverend Talbot stopped by this morning. He invited me to go out and have a pizza with him tonight."

"Reverend Talbot." He repeated the name with curious emphasis. "My, my."

Abbie knew that tone of voice. It always preceded a cross-examination to determine her degree of interest in a particular date.

"Dad, we're just going out for a pizza," Abbie cautioned him not to blow it out of all proportion. It was good advice for herself as well.

"I guess the letter can wait . . . just as long as you retype it first thing in the morning," he decided, and didn't pursue the discussion of her evening date.

"Thanks." Abbie waved him a kiss as she hurried out of the office to her car.

On the surface, it would have seemed more practical to ride back and forth to work with her father, but he was an early riser, often arriving at the office to work at four or five in the morning, when it was quiet and there were no interruptions. Abbie didn't need to be there until the office opened at nine, so she usually drove Mabel.

Mabel grunted her way through the traffic and grumbled up the winding street to Abbie's home. Abbie only had an hour before Seth arrived, and she used every minute of it. While the bathtub filled with water, she ran a dust cloth over the furniture and picked up the clutter of magazines and newspapers.

A quick bath and Abbie was faced with the

impossible decision of what to wear. Nothing seemed exactly appropriate. Her outfits were either too tight, or possibly too revealing, or too plain. Finally she settled on a pair of white jeans and a velour top in a rich kelly-green. Its V-neckline plunged a little. She'd have to remember to sit up straight.

She was just running a brush through her hair when she heard the roar of the sports car's motor coming up the drive. In her haste, she accidentally hooked the bristles in the gold hoop of her earring, giving her ear a painful tug.

"Ouch!" It was a soft, involuntary cry, interrupted by the sound of footsteps on the stairs.

Hurrying out of the bathroom, Abbie reached the door just as he knocked. She opened it, intending to leave with him immediately, but Seth walked in.

"I'm a couple of minutes early. I hope you don't mind," he said, and turned to look at Abbie still holding the door open.

"No, that's all right. I'm ready." She noticed he was wearing his collar. It just peeped over the light blue of his windbreaker.

"This is nice." His glance made an assessing sweep of her apartment. "I wish I had this and you lived in the parsonage." A frown flickered across her face as Abbie wondered whether a minister should be making such comments. Seth read her look, a smile slanting his masculine mouth. "Don't worry. I'm not breaking any commandments. I don't really covet your garret."

"I—"

"You weren't sure," he insisted.

"No."

"You might want to bring a scarf." His glance ran over the coppered blond of her hair. "I've got the top down on my car. The wind's likely to mess up your hair."

"Good idea." There was a nervous edge to her smile as she backed away toward the apartment's small bedroom. "It'll just take me a minute to get one."

"There's no rush," Seth replied.

But Abbie thought otherwise. In her bedroom, she rummaged hurriedly through the top dresser drawer until she found the sheer silk scarf with the green and gold print. The green wasn't the same shade as her velour top but it was close enough.

When she came out, Seth was standing by the table with her typewriter, looking at the stack of handwritten pages beside it. His fingertips were resting on the top paper as if marking a line. A thread of apprehension ran tightly through her edgy nerves.

"Is this the manuscript you're typing?" Seth asked, looking up as if sensing her presence in the room.

"Yes." Abbie tried to remember where she'd left off and what the next scene was that he was reading. Some parts of the book were rather racy.

"I'm glad the Coltrain sisters took my advice," he said, glancing back at the page.

"How did you know?" Abbie stared in stunned wonderment.

"I recognized the handwriting." A hint of a smile made indentations at the corners of his mouth. "Isabel sent me a note. No one else writes with all these flourishes and curlicues." A dark brown eyebrow was arched in query. "Why? Is their identity supposed to be a secret?"

"They asked me not to tell about the book," Abbie admitted.

"Their secret is safe with me," Seth assured her with easy amusement. He tapped a finger on the paper. "Judging by this passage, I think I know why they don't want it known."

"Which passage?" Abbie moved anxiously toward the table and stopped cold when Seth began reading it.

"'His hand cupped her breast and Sophia thought she would surely swoon with pleasure.'" The audible gasp from Abbie prompted him to pause at the end of the sentence, his glance going to her.

"The book really has a good plot," Abbie insisted. "You really shouldn't judge it by that little bit. The characters are interesting and they've done wonderful things with the background."

"I'm not judging it." Laughter and something else gleamed in his eyes. "Did you think I was offended by what I read? Or shocked?"

She bit at the inside of her lower lip, flustered and unnerved. "I don't know," she murmured.

"It can't be your normal reading." Her glance strayed unconsciously to his collar.

"For pleasure, I read mysteries." There was a mocking gleam in his eyes. "Travis McGee is one of my favorite characters. He's had his share of love scenes."

"Oh." Abbie didn't want to pursue this discussion of love and human passions. Sex was the word she was avoiding. She was too conscious they were alone in her apartment. How long had he been up here? Five minutes? Ten? What if her mother or one of the neighbors had noticed? "Maybe we'd better be going," Abbie suggested, clutching the scarf tightly in her hand.

"Of course," he agreed, but amusement continued to lurk in his expression as he followed her to the door. Abbie was conscious of the blue study of his eyes. "How long has it been since you've had a man in your apartment?" Seth asked, just as they reached the door to the stairwell.

She was startled into turning. "Not since—" Abbie almost said, not since she broke up with Jim, but there wasn't any reason to be so specific. "Not for quite a while," she answered instead, and took the door key from her purse.

"I thought you seemed ill at ease." Seth waited at the top of the steps while she locked the door. "Not many people do that around here," he observed, then explained, "Lock their doors when they leave."

"It's a habit left over from living in the city,"

she admitted as she returned the key to her purse and moved to the stairs to join him.

It was a wide stairwell, wide enough for both of them to descend side by side. The touch of his hand on the back of her waist almost stopped Abbie, not quite ready for such casual familiarity. Its warmth electrified her nerve ends and made her overly conscious of his masculine form, lean, muscled, and tall next to her. He didn't take his hand away when they reached the bottom, remaining to guide her to the passenger side of the car. Then Seth moved ahead to open the car door for her.

"Sometimes the latch is stubborn." He used the inside door handle to open it and waited while she climbed in, then pushed it securely shut.

It was a small car, the bucket seats set closely together and a stick shift on the floorboard between them. The close quarters were made even more so when Seth slid behind the wheel, his shoulder nearly touching hers. Abbie tried to hide her awareness of it by busily tying the scarf under her chin. Seth made no attempt to start the motor until she was finished.

"All set?" he asked. Abbie turned her head to nod affirmatively to him and received the full force of his gaze as he made a thorough study of her face. "Your eyes look more green in that color."

There was a crazy little lurching of her stomach. It was so difficult to keep this friendly outing in perspective that Abbie wished he hadn't noticed the way she looked. Compliments put it on a different level, more personal.

"Thank you . . . Reverend." Abbie needed to establish his profession in her mind and somehow keep it there.

His expression took on a thoughtful quality before he turned his profile to her and started the car. The powerful motor growled instantly to life. His hand closed on the gearshift knob and accidentally brushed her knee when he shifted into reverse.

He laid his arm along the top of her seat back as he partially turned to back the car out of the driveway. His carved features didn't seem to have any expression now. Abbie tried to relax now that all his attention was on driving.

The roar of the engine and the wind generated by the car's motion fairly well negated any attempt at conversation. Abbie kept her eyes to the front and her knees out of the way of his constant gearshifting.

The low-built sports car zipped down the winding, tree-shaded streets that *never* crossed at right angles with another. Throughout the hillside town, there were miles of gray stone walls to terrace and hold the steeply sloping earth. Seth avoided the business route through the historic downtown area and turned east on the main highway.

When they arrived at the pizza parlor, the parking lot was relatively full, but there were two empty tables inside. Seth directed her to the one secluded in a quiet corner. Abbie was undecided whether he had chosen it for the privacy it afforded or to avoid being noticed, aware that there was only a fine difference between the two reasons, but a telling one.

There were four chairs around the red-checkered cloth-topped table. After Abbie was seated, Seth pulled out the chair on her right for himself. Once they had ordered, Seth began talking. Before she knew it, there was an easy flow of conversation between them. She stopped being so self-conscious with him and began responding to his friendly manner.

"You can have the last slice of pizza, Abbie." Seth pushed the cardboard circle toward her but she leaned back from the table, shaking her head in refusal.

"I'm so stuffed I can't eat another bite, Reverend," she insisted. "It was really good, though. Thank you."

"You're welcome." He accepted with a mocking tip of his head. "Would you like anything else, Abbie? Another soft drink?"

"No." She reached for her glass, a third full yet. "I have plenty."

There was a moment of silence as he watched her take a sip of the cola through the plastic straw. His glance slid from her mouth to her eyes when she looked up.

"You don't go out much socially do you, Abbie?" It was in the way of an observation more than a question.

She nervously stirred the ice in her drink with the straw. "As much as I want." Abbie defended her lack of an active social life, quietly insisting it was by choice.

"What about close friends?" he asked.

"I was gone for four years and you sort of lose touch," she admitted. "Most of them are married now, with their own families to look after, or else they've moved away. But I'm not lonely, Reverend." She wanted that clear because she didn't want him feeling sorry for her. "I guess I like my own company." She made light of it with a quick smile.

"Or you're just not ready to commit yourself to a close relationship so soon after breaking up with that man in Kansas City," he suggested.

Abbie went a little white. "How did you know about Jim?"

"I could pretend that I was only guessing you'd been hurt recently by a man," Seth replied with a half-shrug. "I suspected it but—in a small town—you find out anyway. Were you very much in love with him?"

"No. I thought I was." She set the glass on the table, her tension growing. It was something she hadn't discussed with anyone. She wasn't sure if she wanted to tell him about it either. Actually there was very little to tell. "But I got over him too quickly, so I guess it wasn't the 'real' thing."

"What happened?"

"Nothing." Abbie discovered a twisted humor in the very appropriate answer. "I was ready to get serious and he wasn't. It was a relationship that had nowhere to go and nothing to keep it going, so it ended."

"I'm glad there aren't any lasting scars." His look was gentle yet contained a certain strength. Loud, laughing voices came from the front of the pizza parlor where there were young people standing. Seth glanced their way, then back to Abbie. "It's beginning to fill up in here. Maybe we should leave so someone can have our table."

Abbie signaled her agreement by pushing her chair back from the table to stand up. His questions concerning her abortive romance kept buzzing around in her mind as they left the restaurant. She began to suspect that was the reason he had invited her out. She had to know, so she wouldn't foolishly think there was another reason.

"Reverend . . ." Abbie slowed her steps when they neared the car. Impatience flickered in his eyes as he paused to meet her steady look. ". . . did you ask me out tonight because you thought I was suffering from a broken heart and needed some consoling?"

A startled frown crossed his forehead. "That never occurred to me, Abbie," he denied, and she doubted that he could have faked that reaction. She felt immensely better, smiling her thanks when he opened the car door for her. He walked around the back of the car and climbed into the driver's side. "I promised to take you straight home, but it looks like we're going to have a beautiful sunset tonight." Seth nodded to the western sky and the pink glow already tinting the clouds. "Would you like to drive up to the lookout and watch it?"

"Yes, I would." Abbie suddenly wasn't in any hurry to go back to her empty apartment.

They weren't far from the lookout point with its overview of Eureka Springs. Its location on the east end of town provided them with the ideal vantage point to observe the glowing colors of sundown.

Seth stopped the car at the farthest edge, facing the west. Turning the ignition off, he combed his fingers through his wind-rumpled hair to restore it to some semblance of order. The hush of twilight seemed to spill over Abbie, the warmth of a summer breeze softly stirring the air. She untied the scarf and let it slide from her hair, while a purpling pink streaked with red painted the horizon.

"It seems too beautiful to be real, doesn't it?" She half glanced at Seth.

"It can be like that," he agreed, and stretched his arm along her seat back. "If an artist tried to put it on canvas, it would look artificial."

"That's true." Abbie realized that her voice was barely above a murmur and laughed softly. "Why are we talking so quietly?"

"Probably because we're the only ones here." Seth smiled. His glance swept the lookout area. "That probably won't be true once it gets dark. This looks like the ideal place for teenagers to park and make out." He tipped his head at Abbie. "Is this where they come?"

"It . . . used to be the local lovers' lane," Abbie admitted, unsettled by the thought.

"Did you ever come here with your boyfriend?" He was mocking her hint of embarrassment.

"A few times, but that was several years ago, Reverend," she replied.

"Will you stop calling me Reverend every time you turn around?" he declared on a note of amused exasperation. "I do have a name, you know. It's Seth."

"I know, Reverend—" she began, suddenly uncertain.

Her pulse rocketed at the silencing finger he placed on her lips. "Seth," he corrected firmly.

She was so tied up in knots she couldn't breathe. He was leaning toward her, his other hand resting on the curve of her shoulder. She felt drawn into the dark aqua depths of his eyes. When his finger slid across her lips in a near caress, a quiver of longing trembled through her.

"Say it," he ordered huskily.

His gaze shifted to her lips to watch them form his name. "Seth," Abbie whispered.

His head bent toward her and she knew instinctively that he was going to kiss her. The tips of his fingers rested lightly along her jaw and the curve of her throat, holding her motionless with no pressure. Excitement danced through her senses, but Abbie willed them to stay under control.

The first brush of his lips was soft and teasing, but they came back to claim her mouth with warm ease. Abbie was hesitant to respond, unwilling to have him discover how much she wanted this, but he coaxed a response from her.

Her lips were clinging to his by the time he finally drew back a few inches to study the result. Slowly her lashes lifted to show the dazed uncertainty of her eyes. Her lips remained slightly parted, melted into softness by his persuasive mouth. She was motionless, but inside she was straining to be closer to him. Abbie was too unsure of herself—and him—to take the initiative. His heavily lidded gaze noted all this with satisfaction.

"Seth?" The rising inflection of her voice put a question mark at the end of his name.

His mouth curved in a compelling smile that seemed to take her breath away. "You've finally got it right, Abbie," Seth murmured, and started to close the distance between them again.

Her lips were moving to meet him halfway when the moment was shattered by the roar of another car approaching the lookout. Abbie abruptly pulled back to cast an anxious glance over her shoulder. His hand came away from the side of her neck and rested on the softness of her upper arm as if he expected her to bolt from the car. The other vehicle wasn't in sight yet, but the roar of its unmuffled engine was coming steadily closer.

Seth hung his head and cursed under a heavy sigh, "Devil damn." Then he was squaring around to place both hands on the wheel.

"What did you say?" Abbie looked at him, her eyes narrowing in bewilderment.

There was a wryness in the sidelong look he sent her. "Devil damn." One corner of his mouth was pulled up. "I had a grandfather who was Danish. Whenever he was upset or angry, that's the expression he used—devil damn or devil damn it. It's much better than breaking a Commandment and taking the Lord's name in vain."

A tremulous smile touched her mouth, inwardly thrilled that he was upset by the interruption. "Yes, it is," Abbie agreed softly.

He held her gaze for a long second that seemed filled with all sorts of heady promises. With another sigh, he reached to turn the key in the ignition just as a car full of teenagers drove into the lookout area.

"I guess I'd better get you home," he said.

While he backed onto the road, Abbie tied the scarf over her hair once more. She felt so good inside that she felt like singing, which of course she didn't do. More than once during the drive home through the back streets, she was conscious of Seth glancing at her. Maybe because she kept stealing looks at him.

Stopping the car in front of the garage, Seth switched off the engine. Abbie waited until he had walked around the car to open her door. He took her hand to help her climb out of the low car.

"I enjoyed myself this evening. Thanks for asking," Abbie said, letting her hand stay in his grasp a moment longer.

"It was *my* pleasure," Seth replied. "I'll walk you to the door."

"There's no need for you to walk me up that flight of steps," she assured him.

"Suit yourself." He shrugged with a mocking look. "I only suggested it because I thought it might bother you if I kissed you good night here—where your parents or the neighbors might see us." When Abbie released a laughing breath of shock at his statement, Seth chuckled and asked, "Would you like to change your mind?"

"It isn't fair to ask a girl that," Abbie protested, because if she said yes, it meant she wanted him to kiss her, and if she said no, it wouldn't be true, but at least she wouldn't sound so brazen.

"I see." The dimpling corners of his mouth were mocking her as he curved an arm along the back of her waist and guided her in the direction of the roofed stairwell. "A man is supposed to walk the girl to the door and take his chances."

"Something like that," she admitted, slipping off the scarf and absently fluffing the ends of her hair.

Her heart was tripping all over her ribs as they climbed the stairs. She didn't know what any of this meant or where these feelings would lead. It was too soon to know. But she liked this glow she felt when he walked beside her like this.

"Do you have your key?" Seth asked when they reached the top of the stairs.

"Yes." Abbie opened her purse and slipped the scarf inside before taking out her key ring.

When she had produced it, his hands settled onto the rounded bones of her shoulders, so she faced him. The width of his chest was in front of her, his head inclined at an angle toward her while his magnetically blue eyes held her rapt attention.

"What do you think my chances are?" he asked with a sensual curve to his hard, male mouth.

It was so easy to sway toward him, her head automatically tilting upward to provide him with the answer. The pressure of his hands increased to bring her nearer. A second before his mouth moved onto hers, a little voice inside warned Abbie that she was kissing a minister and not to respond too wantonly.

But it wasn't an easy warning to heed, not when the soft curves of her body came in contact with the hard contours of his male form, and she was reminded of the differences between the sexes. Her hands slid tentatively around his lean middle, while the breadth of his hands glided down her spine to hold her firmly.

His mouth did not explore this time, already having discovered the warm softness of her lips. There was more depth to his kiss, more subtle demand, less warmth and more fire. Abbie felt the stirrings of desire coming to life within her and pulled reluctantly away before she shocked him with her behavior.

It was difficult to breathe naturally, especially when his arms continued to encircle her and she could still feel the muscled solidness of his thighs brushing against her legs. The moist warmth of his breath was near her cheekbone. Abbie glanced at his face through the top of her lashes, then lowered it to the white collar showing above the black dickey.

"Thank you again, Rev . . . Seth," Abbie corrected herself.

He slowly brought his hands from around her and let a distance come between them. "Good night, Abbie."

"Good night," she returned the farewell. "I'll see you Sunday."

Seth paused on the first step to add, "If not before."

There was a hint of a promise there, even if it wasn't anything definite. She was smiling as she unlocked the door to her apartment, listening to the sound of his footsteps on the stairs.

Chapter Six

"Well?" Her father leaned against her desk and swung a leg over a corner to half sit on it. Abbie moved her cup of coffee to the side so he wouldn't accidentally knock it over.

"Well, what?" she asked with a frown. "Was there something wrong with that letter I just retyped for you?"

"Not a thing. I'm waiting for you to tell me how your date with Reverend Talbot went last night," he said.

Abbie avoided his gaze and began arranging the papers on her desk in neat stacks. "It wasn't a date exactly. But I had a good time—if that's what you're asking."

"A good time." The corners of his mouth were pulled down. "Funny, I had the man pegged as the kind capable of arousing more of a reaction than just a good time."

"Dad, he's a minister," she protested, knowing full well he was right.

"He's a man—made of flesh and blood, just

like the rest of us. Don't put him on a pedestal, Abbie." He studied her more closely. "Are you going to see him again?"

"I imagine." She nodded, then slid him a twinkling glance. "At church on Sunday."

"You know what I meant, did he ask you out again?" her father chided her for being facetious.

Abbie could answer truthfully, "No."

Her father thought about that for a minute and studied his empty coffee cup. "I guess a minister doesn't have a lot of free evenings, what with church youth groups, choir practices, and the civic functions he's expected to attend. It's bound to limit his social life."

"I hadn't thought about it." There was reassurance in it, though, because it offered a possible explanation why Seth hadn't been more definite about when he would see her again.

"Well." He slapped his leg and pushed off her desk. "Guess I'd better get some coffee and get back to my office so you can get some work done."

On Thursday, Abbie left the office early for lunch so she could stop by the post office and send out some registered mail. When she returned a few minutes before one o'clock, her father stuck his head out the door of his private office.

"Reverend Talbot stopped by to see you," he informed her. "He came shortly after you left."

Frustration clouded her expression. This was

the first indication that he had meant to see her before Sunday—and she had missed him.

"Did he say what he wanted?" she asked, feigning a mild interest.

"I guess he wanted to take you to lunch." Her father appeared to be a little vague on that point. "He did say he'd try to catch you another time."

"Oh." Another indefinite. "Thanks, Dad." Abbie sat down to her desk and stowed her purse in the drawer, trying not to be too disappointed.

Saturday morning, Abbie was up early, gathering up her dirty clothes and linen and driving to the laundromat to do her washing. Her mother had offered to let Abbie use her automatic washer and dryer to do her laundry, but it usually took the better part of a day, washing one load at a time. At the laundromat, it usually took just over an hour. Since she would have insisted on paying her mother for the use of the machines anyway, Abbie preferred the time she saved at the laundromat to the convenience of running next door, as it were.

With the laundry finished, she stopped at the grocery store on her way home and picked up the few items she needed. It was going on eleven when she turned Mabel into the driveway. Abbie stepped out of the car, juggling the sack of groceries while she searched her purse for the door key.

"Abbie!" Her mother called from the back stoop of the house. "You had some phone calls while you were gone. They called here when they didn't get any answer."

"Who called?" she frowned.

"Isabel Coltrain. She didn't say what she wanted, but she seemed very anxious to talk to you." Her mother was consumed with curiosity. "Do you have any idea what she might have wanted?"

To see if Abbie had finished the last stack of manuscript pages the sisters had given her? But Abbie had kept her word to the women. "Maybe it had something to do with typing," she said in a half-truth. "The word has spread that I'm doing typing on the side. I've gotten several calls."

"But what would they want typed?"

"Who knows?" Abbie shrugged to avoid an outright lie, and turned again toward the garage.

The acceleration of a car engine as it turned into the driveway pulled her glance over her shoulder. A dark green sports car zoomed toward her, its racy appearance making it seem to travel faster than it actually was. Excitement leaped along her veins when she recognized the car and the driver, and turned to meet them.

"I forgot to tell you," her mother called belatedly. "Reverend Talbot phoned, too." When he turned off the engine and vaulted out of the car, her mother explained to him, "I was just telling Abbie that you called for her."

"That's all right, Mrs. Scott. Thanks." Seth nodded to the woman, then walked toward Abbie with an easy, rolling stride. He was wearing Levi's again, and a blue chambray shirt opened at the throat—with no collar.

"I just got back." The gladness she was trying to contain shined in the emerald-green flecks of her hazel eyes.

"So I gathered. Here." He reached for the grocery sack. "Let me carry that for you."

Her resistance took only a token form as she relinquished the sack into his arms and walked to the stairway door. "I'm sorry I missed you Thursday, Reverend. Dad said you stopped by."

"Are we going to start that again?" Seth challenged.

"Start what?" Abbie paused on the first step.

"That Reverend business." The dark intensity of his gaze made her blood warm.

"I call 'em as I sees 'em." She mocked him with a provocative glance. Immediately she was attacked by pangs of self-consciousness that she had actually been flirting with him.

"Look, Abbie." He touched the tanned hollow of his throat with his free hand. "No collar. For the rest of the day, you're looking at Seth. So you be sure to call him the way you see him."

"All right—Seth," she agreed, her tone a little more subdued.

"Do you have anything on your day's agenda?" Seth asked as he mounted the stairs one step behind her.

"The Coltrain sisters are getting anxious. I was going to do some more typing on their manuscript," Abbie explained.

"It's a fine August day. What you need is fresh air and sunshine—not more hours in front of a typewriter," he insisted. "I'm here to unchain you from that."

"You are?" Abbie unlocked the door and pushed it open, walking in ahead of Seth. She was alive with pleasure. The realization that he wanted to spend the day with her swelled within her, but she didn't want to appear too eager, too overjoyed.

"Yes, I am." Seth walked to the counter-bar on the kitchen side of the room and set the grocery sack on it.

Abbie moved to the opposite side to begin putting the groceries away. The brilliance of his dark gaze was difficult to meet. There was something possessive about it that started a fire licking along her veins.

"You'll have to give me a few minutes to change clothes after I get these groceries put away," she said.

His eyes made a lazy inspection of the faded blue jeans softly hugging her slim hips and the thin white blouse with its capped sleeves and half-collar. Her auburn-gold hair was pulled back in a ponytail, a white silk scarf tied around it.

"What you're wearing is perfect," Seth insisted.

They were everyday clothes, clean but showing the wear and thinness of many washings. Abbie looked down at them, then back at Seth. If her present clothes were suitable for the occasion, it raised a question. "Where are we going?" She tipped her head to the side.

His strongly shaped mouth slanted in a half-smile. "Heaven."

"What?" Abbie blinked.

"I should have said, heaven on earth," he conceded, with the richness of amusement deepening his voice. "I found a quiet, little spot in the country. It's peaceful, beautiful—the perfect place for a picnic."

"A picnic." She smiled at the initial appeal of the idea, then became serious as she began to think about what food she had in the apartment that she could fix.

Seth appeared to read her thoughts. "I already have a picnic basket filled with more food than we can possibly eat. It's sitting in the back of my car. You don't have to worry about fixing a thing."

"Isn't there anything I can bring?" she asked.

"Just yourself." His gaze claimed her with a vibrancy that made Abbie feel shaky inside.

"All right." Her voice was tinged with a soft breathlessness as she let herself drift under his persuasive spell.

The telephone started ringing, its shrillness making a sharp intrusion between them. Abbie bit her lip in indecision and glanced at the ringing phone.

"That has to be one of the Coltrain sisters," she murmured and wondered what excuse she could give them for not having any more of their manuscript typed.

"I'll answer it." Seth was already moving toward the phone when he spoke.

"Oh, but—" Abbie started to protest, taking a step after him.

But Seth already had his hand on the receiver. He sent her a backward glance over his shoulder. "You get those groceries put away so we can leave," he ordered. "I'll handle the sisters for you."

Abbie gripped the sides of the cardboard milk container she had taken from the sack and watched anxiously as Seth picked up the phone. What would the sisters think when he answered her phone?

"Miss Scott's residence," he said into the mouthpiece and paused. "She's busy at the moment. This is Reverend Talbot. May I help you, Miss Coltrain?" He glanced over his shoulder and noticed Abbie just standing there.

His mouth curved into a wry line as he motioned her to get busy. Without taking her anxious gaze from him, Abbie moved sideways to the refrigerator and opened the door to set the milk inside.

"No, she hasn't finished the typing for you," he said into the phone. "Miss Scott planned to type more today, but I have decided she's been working too hard, so I'm taking her out for the balance of the day." Seth half turned from the waist up to send a smiling look at Abbie and nod in response to the voice on the other end of the line. "I knew you'd understand, Miss Coltrain."

There was another short pause. "Yes, I'll tell her. Good-bye."

Abbie quickly pushed the loaf of bread into the bread drawer as Seth replaced the receiver on its cradle and crossed to the counter. Her glance bounced off his masculine features.

"What did she say?" she murmured.

"Isabel apologized for rushing you about the manuscript and hoped you weren't too exhausted by all the typing you've done for them." Seth relayed the message. "She thought the outing was an excellent idea."

Abbie turned away to put the box of cereal in the cupboard. "But didn't she . . ." She didn't finish the question, concerned that she might be too sensitive and guilty of overreacting.

". . . didn't she think it strange that I answered the phone?" Seth completed the sentence, almost verbatim to what was in her mind. "Why should she?" he countered evenly when Abbie turned with a guilty start. "It's normal for a minister to call on members of his congregation in their homes."

"Yes, but . . ." She couldn't finish that sentence either.

". . . but you are a young and very attractive single woman." Again Seth accurately guessed the rest of it. "And I'm a bachelor."

"Something like that, yes," Abbie admitted.

"As romantically inclined as those two spinster sisters are, I'd guess they're tittering with the possibility a romance is developing between us." A suppressed smile deepened the corners of his mouth as he met her startled look.

"Oh." This small response was all she could manage, since he had confirmed exactly what she had guessed they'd be thinking.

"We lunched together, had pizza one evening, and now we're going on a picnic together," Seth reminded her. "It isn't unlikely that an outsider would jump to that conclusion."

"I know." Abbie nodded.

With calm deliberation, Seth walked around the counter-bar and took the sack of sugar out of her hands, setting it on the countertop. Her protest died when his hands moved over the bareness of her upper arms with caressing ease.

"Why bother to deny it?" Seth challenged softly while he looked deeply into her eyes. A shiver of sensations slivered through her veins. "It's true, isn't it?"

"I—suppose." The whispered admission was hesitant; she was wary of declaring too openly the feelings that were growing stronger with each meeting.

He tipped his head to one side, bronze lights darkening his hair. The expression on his roughly carved features mildly taunted her for her cautious reply, while his hands continued their slow, lazy kneading of her arms.

"You don't sound too sure," he said. "If this isn't the start of a romance, what else would you call it?"

"I don't know," Abbie admitted with an uncertain smile.

"What's the matter?" Seth asked. "Why does it bother you to admit it?"

"I guess I'm not used to being so candid," she suggested, then deliberately tried to side-track the conversation. "How did the Coltrain sisters find out that you knew about their manuscript?"

The faintly mocking glitter in his eyes informed her that Seth knew why she was changing the subject. "They invited me to dinner Tuesday night. I mentioned that we had been together the previous night and that I'd read a couple pages of the manuscript you were typing without revealing that I had recognized their handwriting," he explained. "They were so eager to find out my reaction that they confessed they had written it and asked what I thought." His smile became more pronounced. "So they don't think that you betrayed their secret."

"I wondered," she acknowledged.

"I also promised them I'd write a letter to some friends of mine in the publishing business and see what I could do to help them when it's finished." He let his hands come away from her arms and turned to look in the grocery sack. "Is there anything else in here that's perishable?"

"No, I've already put those items away." There were only some canned goods left.

"Then, let's leave the rest and go on our picnic," he stated.

"Okay." Abbie had the feeling she would agree to almost anything he suggested.

Within minutes after leaving town, Seth turned off the main highway onto a graveled county road that twisted along the ridges and hollows. Abbie was completely lost, having no idea where they were going. She'd never done that much exploring of the countryside to be familiar with all the hill roads.

The August heat had seared the grasses a golden brown to intersperse the thickly forested hills with patches of bright color. Abbie turned her face into the blowing force of the wind generated by the sports car, kicking up plumes of dust on the graveled road.

An azure sky contained a scattering of powder-puff clouds, drifting slowly while the golden sun-ball blazed above the earth with its light. Overhead, a hawk circled, floating effortlessly on the air currents. They were riding on a ridgeback, the Ozark Mountains undulating into the distance like ocean waves.

There was a change in the powerful hum of the engine as Seth eased the pressure on the accelerator slowing the car. A fairly straight stretch of road lay before them with no roads branching off it. All Abbie could see was a short lane leading to the gate of a fenced field, but it appeared to be Seth's destination as he braked the car to a slower speed to make the turn onto it. When the car was stopped, he switched off the engine, removing the sunglasses he'd been wearing.

"This is it," he said with a glance at Abbie while he pushed his door open to step out.

Abbie looked at the gate and the sign tacked on the post that very plainly read: PRIVATE PROPERTY—Trespassers Will Be Prosecuted. "We aren't going into that field, are we?" She climbed out of the passenger side, but eyed Seth with a bewildered frown.

The nearly bald knoll had only a scattering of tall oak trees to shade its yellow grasses. There didn't appear to be any animals grazing in the hill meadow, but the sign on the fence was very definite.

"Wait until you see the view," Seth replied after he had issued an affirmative nod. He reached behind the driver's seat and lifted out a wicker picnic basket. "Do you think you can carry this?"

"But there's a no-trespassing sign on the gate," Abbie pointed out as she took the basket from him and hooked her forearm under the handles. "We can't go in there."

"Yes, we can." Seth removed a Styrofoam cooler from the car's trunk and started walking to the gate. "This land belongs to my family."

"Your family," Abbie repeated with surprise. "I didn't know you had any relation living around here."

"I don't." He stopped at the gate and set the cooler on the ground. There was a padlock on the chain that circled the fence and gatepost. With a key from his pocket, Seth unlocked it and unwrapped the chain to let the gate sag open. "It's a case of absentee ownership, an investment for possible development or resale in the future."

"Oh." But Abbie didn't feel that she knew any more despite the enlightening remark.

"Careful you don't trip on the wire," Seth cautioned as she started to walk through the narrow opening. "I don't want to be responsible for causing a personal injury lawsuit."

It was said in jest but Abbie just wondered all the more. As she went through the gate she was close enough to read the small lettering at the bottom of the sign. The owner was identified as the Tal-bar Corporation. "The Tal-bar Corporation belongs to your family?" she asked when Seth followed her, leaving the gate open behind him.

"Yes. It's a combination of Talbot and Barlow. Barlow was my grandmother's maiden name, and her brother was one of the original partners with my grandfather," he explained. "I thought we'd have our picnic under that oak tree over there." Seth indicated the closest one with a nod of his head.

"Is it a big company?" Abbie suspected it was, since it had landholdings in the Ozarks.

"For a family-owned company, I'd say it's fairly large, but it's certainly not a major national corporation." There was a dry amusement in his tone.

"I guess your family mentioned they owned some land here when you were assigned to our church," Abbie guessed.

"Actually I was here a few years when we originally bought this property, so I was a little familiar with the area before I obtained my transfer."

"You aren't active in your family's company, are you?" Abbie frowned, automatically stopping under the tree when Seth did. She didn't see how it was possible when he was a minister. Yet his remark about looking at the property seemed to indicate otherwise.

"My father insists that I remain on the board of directors to act as their conscience," Seth admitted as he crouched down to set the cooler next to the tree. "There's a small blanket in your basket. We can spread it on the ground."

While she digested the information, Abbie opened the lid of the wicker basket and took out the square blanket lying on top of the plastic dishes. She shook it out and laid it out flat on the grass-stubbled ground. Kneeling on it, she began taking the dishes and utensils out of the basket. "I know it's none of my business . . ." But she couldn't help prying a little more into his personal affairs. ". . . but I have the feeling your father would have preferred that you had joined the company. . . ."

"Instead of becoming a minister?" Seth completed what she had left unsaid. There was a light shrug of his shoulders as he began taking out containers of assorted salads. "In the beginning, he was against the idea—until he was convinced that it was definitely what I wanted. I've had his full support and his blessing for several years now—as well as from the rest of my family."

She was glad that Seth's chosen profession had not created any friction between him and his family, but it sounded too trite to say so. The removal of the napkins and the salt and pepper shakers emptied the picnic basket. Abbie sat in the grass out of the way.

"We have here a private buffet." Seth indicated the various uncovered containers arranged in a semicircle on the blanket. "Macaroni salad, potato salad, ambrosia, tomato aspic, cold roast chicken, ham, fresh fruit, cheese. There's a couple things that I don't know what they're called."

Abbie stared at the array of food. "You don't expect us to eat all this?"

There was a wicked glint in his eye. "To tell you the truth, it was the quickest way to clean out my refrigerator. The ladies in the community have been more than generous about bringing me samples of their cooking."

"Maybe they thought it was the way to win the favor of a bachelor minister," Abbie suggested with a hint of a teasing smile.

"'The way to a man's heart . . .'" Seth followed her thinking and chuckled. "Unfortunately, they couldn't know that I had already been tempted by a copper-haired girl on the road, who gave me fruit." He paused a second to hold Abbie's glance. "There are some who believe that it was the peach, not the apple, Adam and Eve ate in the Garden of Eden."

"Really," she murmured, a little unnerved by the sensuality of his look, so vibrant and alive with his male interest in her.

"Yes, really," he mocked, and turned to reach inside the cooler. "Don't you think you have what it takes to tempt me into sin?"

"Are you sure it's not the other way around?" Abbie countered, matching his sexual banter and not letting him see how much it disturbed her.

There was a heartiness to his throaty chuckle. "I deserved that. You know the right way to put a man in his place, don't you, Abbie?" Seth didn't appear to expect an answer as he took a bottle of chilled wine from the cooler. "Now, this happens to come from my own private stock. It's not a gift from anyone."

Abbie looked at him askance. "Are you allowed to drink wine?"

There was patience in his strong face as he uncorked the bottle and splashed a small portion of wine in two glasses. "In the Book of Matthew, Jesus explains in chapter fifteen that it is not what goes into the mouth that defiles man, but what comes out of his mouth. 'Whatever goes into the mouth passes into the stomach, and so passes on, but what comes out of the mouth proceeds from the heart. . . .'" he paused. "Anything in excess is not good for the body—sweets, fats, or alcohol."

"That's true," she agreed, taking the glass he handed her.

"In biblical times, they drank wine with their meals because the water wasn't potable, for the most part," he added. "It was the fruit of the vine that Jesus gave to his disciples at the Last Supper. That's hardly a justification for the consumption of alcohol. But there's a vast difference between drinking and having an occasional glass of wine with a meal."

"I agree." Abbie swirled the rose-red liquid in her glass. "I wasn't really criticizing you for bringing the wine."

"Weren't you?" It was a mild accusation.

"No, although it probably sounded like it," she admitted with a rueful laugh.

"Sometimes I get the feeling you are more pious than I am," Seth mocked. "No deviating from the straight and narrow."

"I've never been very well acquainted with a minister—on a personal basis." Abbie defended some of her preconceived notions. "So I don't always know what to expect."

"I have noticed." He nodded, a faint smile touching the corners of his mouth. "Right now, you're wondering if I'm going to say a blessing before we eat."

"I was," Abbie admitted on a note of bubbling laughter.

When Seth bowed his head, Abbie did, too. "We thank you, O Lord, for this bounty You have placed before us. And we pray that You will also feed the hunger of our hearts with the Grace of Your Love. Amen."

"Amen," she echoed softly, and lifted her head to glance at him in silent wonder, touched by the simple blessing.

"Shall we dig in?" Seth murmured, arching an eyebrow in her direction, and passed her the small bowl of potato salad.

Chapter Seven

Although Abbie had only taken a small sample of everything, there had been too many dishes. There was still some food left in her plate, but she didn't have room for another bite.

"I think it's a case of my eyes being bigger than my stomach." She sighed and set her fork on the plate.

"There's a lot of wildlife around here that will eat it, so it won't go to waste." Seth rolled to his feet. "If you're finished, I'll scrape your plate on that stump so the scraps won't be attracting the flies around us."

"I am finished." Abbie handed him the plate.

While he walked to the tree stump about twenty yards away, she started putting the lids on the containers and returning them to the cooler so they wouldn't spoil. When Seth came back, he lent a hand, stowing the dishes and silverware in the wicker basket. Once the blanket was cleared and shaken free of any crumbs, Abbie shifted to sit near the middle of it, leaning on her hands and stretching her legs out to ease the fullness of her stomach. Before she could guess his intention, Seth was lying down at right angles to her, with his head resting on her lap.

"Do you mind me using you for a pillow?" Seth looked up at her with deceptively innocent eyes, aware of asking permission after the fact.

"No." But she did find it disturbingly intimate. Her senses were operating on an uneven keel with his head nestled against her thighs. The faded material of her jeans had been worn thin, providing a scant barrier for her sensitive skin.

"Good." Seth closed his eyes and settled more comfortably in place, folding his hands across his chest in a gesture of contentment.

With his eyes shut, Abbie took the liberty of studying the irregular angles and planes of his strong face. There was power in the lift of his cheekbones and steady determination in the clean line of his jaw. His stubby lashes were dark and full, a shade darker than the brown of his eyebrows. There was a slight, crooked break in the line of his nose, and his mouth was well defined, neither too thin nor too full, and definitely masculine.

The dark, rumpled gold of his hair invited the smoothing touch of her fingers. Abbie curled them into the blanket to resist the urge to slide them through his hair. The body heat from his wide shoulders warmed the side of her hip and thigh and spread through the rest of her body. All sorts of dangerous thoughts were running through her mind when she let her glance stray to the even rise and fall of his chest. Starting a conversation seemed the wise thing to do.

"Where does your family live, Seth?" she asked.

A little frown creased his forehead. "Pillows aren't supposed to talk," he grunted.

Abbie laughed softly at that. "Well, this pillow does," she retorted. "Where does your family live?"

He sighed in mock resignation. "My parents live in Denver."

"Is that where the Tal-bar Corporation has its offices, too?"

"Yes."

"How did the company get started?" she asked.

Seth opened one eye. "My, but you are full of questions."

"How else do you learn anything?" Abbie reasoned with a small shrug.

"My grandfather and great-uncle started out as well drillers, then got into the oil and gas business, and backed into cattle ranching."

" 'Backed' into cattle ranching? How do you do that?" Abbie smiled at the phrase, finding it curious.

"My grandfather thought he was acquiring the mineral rights for federal land and found out he had actually obtained grazing rights instead. So he and my great-uncle turned a mistake into a business," Seth explained. "The company also has some mining interest."

"Do you have any brothers or sisters?" she wondered.

"A whole houseful." He sat up unexpectedly, and turned toward Abbie, bracing a hand on the opposite side of her legs. "I have five sisters and three brothers. My parents believed in a large family. Do you like large families?"

"Yes." Her answer was hesitant because she wasn't sure what he meant by the question.

Seth took it a step farther. "How many children do you want when you get married?"

"That's something . . . I'd have to discuss with my husband." She had trouble breathing when he leaned closer. Her heart started fluttering against her ribs.

"What would you say . . ." He tipped his head to kiss the side of her throat. There was a wild, little leap of her pulse. ". . . if your husband wanted . . ." He turned his head to mouth the sensitive cord on the other side of her neck. ". . . a lot of children?"

So many other things were happening in reaction to his nuzzling kisses that Abbie almost forgot the question. "I think . . . I'd like the idea." Tension knotted her throat until she couldn't swallow. A moan trembled somewhere inside her, waiting to be released.

"And if he wanted to adopt some children . . ." His mouth grazed along her cheek, feathering her skin with the warmth of his breath. ". . . in addition to your own?"

"Why not?" she murmured, turning her head to end the tantalizing nearness of his mouth.

It moved onto her lips with a sureness of purpose, claiming them as if it had long been his right to do so. There was no resistance to its commanding pressure. Her lips parted willingly to deepen the kiss as his hand curved itself to her spine. A heady tide of feeling seemed to swamp her, and she reeled at the whirling mist of glorious sensation. She felt drunk with his kiss and wondered if it was the wine.

Then there was no room for thinking, only feeling. Abbie was weightless, floating in a mindless bliss. She wasn't conscious of sinking backward onto the blanket, only that her hands no longer had to support her upright position and were now free to glide around his muscled shoulders and curl into the virile thickness of his hair.

Tiny little moans of pleasure came from her throat when he nibbled sensually at her earlobe and made an intimate study of her neck and throat. The hard contours of his body pressed their male shape onto her flesh while the stroking caress of his hands wandered over her.

Desire seemed a natural extension of all the raw emotion his embrace was disclosing to her. It was the purest form of passion she'd ever know, and the beauty of it swelled her heart until she ached for him. The need inside her strained to be released.

His hand glided smoothly across her ribs, nearing the heated fullness of her breasts. The sensation of skin against skin suddenly shocked her into an awareness of how far out of control she'd gone. Her blouse had fallen loose, the old material stretching to release the lower buttons.

With a stifled moan of panic at what he must be thinking of her, Abbie wiggled from under him and scrambled to her feet. Her breath came thickly as she quickly turned her back to avoid his stunned and frowning look.

"Abbie?" His voice was low and husky.

"I'm sorry." She quickly began stuffing her blouse inside the waistband of her jeans, a task made difficult by her shaking hands. She heard him stand up. "I don't know what got into me," she insisted. "It must have been those two glasses of wine."

His hands closed on her shoulders, the contact momentarily paralyzing. Her blouse was half in and half out, and Abbie couldn't seem to move to finish the job.

"That's not a very flattering thing to say," Seth declared and forced her to turn around. She looked everywhere but into his face, yet the sight of his manly chest, so broad and muscled, hardly hidden at all with his shirt clinging to the heated dampness of his skin, was almost equally unnerving. Abbie kept her hands rigidly tightened into fists so they wouldn't be tempted to touch him.

"I don't know what you mean," she murmured tightly.

"You indicated it was the wine that made you respond to me," he said in a voice that was warm and indulgent. "I was hoping it might have been my kisses."

"It was. I mean . . . I just got carried away because . . . of the wine," Abbie insisted.

Seth crooked a finger under her chin and lifted it to study her face at an angle. "It wasn't because of the wine. You were enjoying being kissed and caressed."

"I was, but . . ." She was close to tears, so anxious for him to think well of her. She had never felt so vulnerable in her life. ". . . I don't want you to think I'm immoral."

"Why should I think that?" Seth questioned with a smiling frown of confusion.

"Because—" Abbie couldn't finish it.

"Because I was touching you? Because I wanted to touch your breasts?" He was even more specific, and his bluntness was more than she could handle. "Or because you wanted me to?"

"Seth." She shut her eyes so he couldn't read how right he was in her look.

"I'm relieved you didn't call me Reverend," he mocked, and gave her a little shake to force her eyes open. "Abbie, I'm a man, not a saint. You are a beautiful woman with a beautiful body. Do you think I don't feel desire when I'm near you?"

"I don't know," she whispered.

"Well, I do." The corners of his mouth deepened with a smile. "Desire isn't necessarily sinful. Promiscuity, infidelity, adultery—those are sinful. Desire is a warm and wonderful thing between two people who care for one another. You don't need to be ashamed of it."

"I wasn't, not really. I just didn't—" She broke

off in midsentence when Seth suddenly began unbuttoning his shirt and pulling it loose from his Levi's. "What are you doing?"

"I'm unbuttoning my shirt. What does it look like I'm doing?" he countered. "You seemed embarrassed because your blouse came unfastened. I thought it might make you feel better if mine was loose, too."

"Seth, that's ridiculous." Abbie couldn't believe he was serious.

His low, throaty laugh vibrated over her. His hands were at her waist to pull her into his arms. That curling sensation started all over again in her stomach as his mouth came down to probe apart the softness of hers. Warmth flooded through her limbs as his molding hands roamed her back and hips to fit her intimately to his hard, male length.

Seth deepened the disruptively sensual embrace with consummate skill, dazzling Abbie with the ecstasy he evoked. Her hands were flattened against his bared chest, absorbing the heat of his body to add to the fire burning inside. She was trembling when he finally lifted his head to trail a butterfly kiss on her closed eyes.

Reluctantly, she started to shift away from him, thinking that he was signaling an end to the embrace, but his arms tightened to keep her fused to the muscled columns of his legs. "Stay here," he murmured, "where you belong."

His hand cupped the back of her head, his fingers tangling with the tendrils of rust-gold hair that had escaped from her ponytail, and firmly directed her head to rest on his shoulder. Of their own volition it seemed, her arms slid around his middle under his loosely hanging shirt. Abbie rested her cheek contentedly against his collarbone, breathing in the heady, male smell of him.

There was a very definite sensation of belonging in his arms. The hard line of his jaw was rubbing against her hair in a sensual caress. With a slight turn of her head, Abbie let her mouth lightly taste the warm flavor of his skin, tanned and tautly stretched across sinew and bone.

Her lips touched the coolness of a gold chain, reminding Abbie of her previous curiosity about it. She shifted slightly in his arms to lift a hand to follow the path of the long chain to where it ended in the center of the springy, silken gold chest hairs. They curled softly against the back of her hand as she held a plain, gold cross between her fingers.

"I wondered what you were wearing around your neck," she admitted softly. The edges were worn, a few scratches dulling the finish. "It looks very old."

"It belonged to my grandfather. He was a very religious man in many ways. And a very passionate man, too." His head tipped slightly downward for a glimpse of her face. "The two can go together."

The sheer naturalness of being held by him had been so overwhelming that it wasn't until his comment that Abbie realized his hand was curved to the underside of her breast, his thumb absently stroking its rising swell. Both her blouse and her cotton brassiere lay between his hand and her flesh, but his touch suddenly seemed to burn through both of them. Abbie stiffened in a delayed attack of modesty.

Guessing the reason, Seth let his hand slide down to the curve of her waist. "I knew what my right hand was doing, so I'm not about to cut it off," he mocked with gentle amusement. "I have the feeling, Abbie, that you are as steeped in Victorian traditions as this town."

Thinking he was ridiculing her for being prudish, Abbie started to pull away, but the bronzed band of his arm stopped her while he cupped his hand to the side of her face and forced her to look at him. There was smoldering pleasure in the darkness of his gaze.

"And I'm glad you are that way," Seth added to assure her that he approved of her keen sense of decorum. "Just remember there will come a time when there is no need to hold back your desires."

"Yes." It seemed very close, too. Abbie hoped, desperately, that she wasn't wrong.

There was a hard, brief kiss before Seth released her from the close contact with his body. "As enjoyable as it would be to idle away the rest of the afternoon kissing you, I think we'd better get our picnic things packed away in the car so we can visit your grandmother."

"Grandmother Klein?" She felt stupid saying

that. She was the only grandmother Abbie had—living that is.

"You usually visit her on the weekend, don't you?" he said. "At the moment, it seems the prudent way to spend the afternoon rather than yielding to the temptation of this blanket and you."

"I think you deliberately try to shock me," Abbie declared, still not quite used to his frankness.

He reached down to scoop up the blanket and begin folding it into a square. His side-glance ran to her, glittering with amusement.

"I have to do something to shatter that sexless image you have of a minister," Seth countered.

"You're succeeding," she admitted, without mentioning that it was something of a revelation.

"It's about time," he replied with a mocking slant to his mouth.

It didn't take long to stow the picnic items in the car. After Abbie had given him a general set of directions to her grandmother's farm, they started out. Less than thirty minutes later, Seth turned the sports car onto the lane leading to the white, clapboard house.

White leghorn chickens squawked and ran from the car with flapping wings when it rolled to a dusty halt in the farmyard. An old gray tomcat sauntered out to inspect the visitors to his territory and meowed an aloof welcome when he recognized Abbie, then eyed Seth with haughty inquiry.

"That's Godfrey." Abbie identified the cat. "He thinks he owns the farm."

"I had the same impression," Seth replied.

"Where's your mistress, Godfrey?" Abbie glanced at the house but there was no sign of life behind the gray-meshed screen door. The cat swished his tail and jumped lithely onto the rear fender of the car to begin cleaning himself, disdaining any notion that he would lower himself to act as guide. "She's probably in the garden," Abbie guessed. "It's around in back."

As Abbie started in that direction, Seth fell into step beside her, his hand fitting itself familiarly to the small of her back. There was something lightly possessive about his touch that made her feel she belonged to him, a sensation she definitely liked.

Just when they entered the fenced yard, a small woman in loose-fitting pants and a flowered blouse came around the corner of the house. The slight stoop to her shoulders was the only visible concession to advanced age. Her short hair was still carrot-red, the result of a regularly applied henna dye. Her sun-leathered complexion was liberally dotted with youthful freckles. She was carrying a five-gallon bucket, loaded full of sweet corn ears, and showing no indication that it was too heavy.

"Hello, Grandmother." Abbie called the greeting.

The woman stopped and waited for them to come to her, but she didn't bother to set the bucket down. Sharp, green eyes made a thorough inspection of Seth, not leaving out a single detail.

"I thought you were probably in the garden," Abbie said. "I wish you wouldn't work out there during the heat of the day."

"I've gotta keep moving at my age," her grandmother insisted, and turned her gaze once more to Seth. "So, you've finally brought a man for me to meet. It's about time." She didn't give either of them a chance to speak as her glance went past them to the dark green sports car. "Is that your car? I always wanted to go tearing down the road in one of those racy convertibles —with my hair flying in the wind. I used to wear it longer, when I was young."

"I'll take you for a ride in it anytime you say, Mrs. Klein," Seth offered with an engaging half-smile. "I'm Seth Talbot."

"I'm pleased to meet you, Seth Talbot," her grandmother replied and looked at Abbie. "You've picked out a strong, virile man. I'll wager he'll have you pregnant a week after you're married."

"Grandmother!" Abbie was aghast. She'd never said things like that before. There had always been the urgings to get married and start a family. Being a farmer's wife, she had always been very casual about the mating habits of animals. Despite this, her grandmother's remark probably wouldn't have struck her as being so scandalous except that—"Seth is a minister."

"So? He's a man, isn't he?" It didn't seem to

make any difference to her grandmother. "He might as well know that I'd like to have a great-grandchild before I die."

"There's plenty of time. You aren't that old," Abbie protested as she sought a tactful way to explain that her grandmother was misreading the situation.

"Considering how long it's taken you to find a suitable man, I wouldn't say there's plenty of time. I was married at seventeen, and had my first baby in my arms when I was eighteen. You're twenty-three years old already, Abbie. You've taken your own sweet time about becoming engaged, let alone married."

"Seth and I aren't engaged, Grandmother," she corrected.

"I thought that's why you brought him out here with you." Her grandmother looked taken aback, and perhaps a little bit embarrassed. "You haven't ever brought a man with you when you've visited me before."

"I was the one who suggested we come here this afternoon," Seth stated, taking the responsibility for the decision. "Abbie had mentioned that she usually visited you on the weekends. Since we had picnicked not far from here, it seemed logical to stop by." He took a step forward, apparently untroubled by the initial conclusion the older woman had reached. "Would you let me carry that sweet corn for you?"

"I can manage it." Her grandmother was a little flustered by her mistake, not liking to appear old and foolish.

FOR THE LOVE OF GOD

"I'm sure you can," Seth agreed easily. "But my father would have my hide if I didn't carry it for you, the way a gentleman should."

Abbie was amazed to see her grandmother surrender the pail of corn to him. Any time she had offered to carry something heavy, her grandmother had impatiently waved her off, insisting she didn't like being fussed over.

"You can set it on the back porch," her grandmother instructed. "Then we'll all go in the house for some cold lemonade."

"These are good-looking roasting ears, Mrs. Klein." Seth complimented her on her garden produce.

"It isn't easy staying one step ahead of the raccoons. Between them and the deer, they play havoc with my garden." She always claimed to have an ongoing battle with the wildlife in the area. "I'll get you a sack, Abbie," she said as they started toward the back door. "So you can take a couple dozen ears of this corn home for you and your folks. You can take some home with you, too, Mr. Talbot. Or should I call you Reverend."

He slid a dryly amused glance at Abbie. "'Seth' will do fine, Mrs. Klein."

When Seth and Abbie walked out of the house more than an hour later, they were each laden with sacks of goods. In addition to the sweet corn, Grandmother Klein had sent along jars of her freshly made tomato preserves and peach butter. She followed them out to the car to bid them good-bye.

"Alice said she was coming out Tuesday to help me put up the corn," Grandmother Klein remarked as Abbie settled into the passenger seat. "Tell her to bring some jar lids."

"I will," Abbie promised.

"Don't forget, Seth, you promised to take me for a ride in this car sometime," her grandmother reminded him.

"How about next Saturday?" Seth suggested, setting a definite time. "You and I can go for a spin while Abbie fixes lunch."

"It sounds like a terrific idea," she agreed in youthful vernacular.

"It's a date." He started the engine and revved it up a few times for the old lady's benefit, then turned the car in a circle in the farmyard to head down the lane. "Your grandmother is quite a woman," he said to Abbie, raising his voice to make himself heard above the noise of the motor.

Abbie responded with an affirmative nod, not attempting to compete with the car or the whipping wind. The noise increased with the acceleration of the engine as they turned onto the state highway and headed for Eureka Springs.

It seemed an exceedingly short ride—and a short day, too, but it was already after five when Seth stopped the car in the driveway. Abbie climbed out of the car and reached for the sack stowed behind the seat.

"I'll carry that up for you," Seth volunteered.

"Thanks, but I'm going to divvy it up with my

138

parents first," Abbie explained and stood awkwardly, holding the sack in her arms. "And I had a wonderful time, and the picnic was delicious." She remembered the last time he'd taken her home and threatened to kiss her in full view of anyone looking. But she hadn't any excuse for going to her apartment, then coming directly down with the sack. It would be just as obvious to anyone watching.

"I'll see you in church tomorrow," he said and bent his head, lightly brushing her lips with his and drawing away before she could react.

It was only after he'd backed out of the drive that Abbie noticed her laundry still sitting in Mabel's backseat. She could have had Seth carry it upstairs for her. It would have been the perfect excuse. She sighed over the lack of foresight.

Her father came out the back door, carrying the kitchen wastebasket. "That was the reverend that just left, wasn't it?"

"Yes. We were out to Grandmother Klein's." She waited near the back door while he emptied the wastebasket into the garbage can. "There's a bunch of sweet corn here for you and Mom."

"Have you been with the reverend all day?" He took the sack out of her arms. "I thought you were in your apartment typing all this time."

"We went for a picnic, then to Grandmother's," she explained.

"Are those bells I hear?" he teased.

"Dad, you're impossible."

"Why?" he countered lightly. "Is the reverend the type that fools around? I've heard Bible salesmen are notorious philanderers. Maybe ministers are too."

"That isn't funny." She didn't want to think that Seth might just be toying with her.

Chapter Eight

The menu lay unopened on the table in front of her. Abbie took another sip from her water glass and glanced at her watch. With the advent of September and the start of school, there was a lull in the tourist trade. She hadn't taken it into account when she left the office early to stop at the post office before meeting Seth for lunch. They had agreed to meet at twelve noon, and it was still five minutes before the hour.

In the last month, she'd seen him on a fairly regular basis. They usually lunched together twice a week and went out to dinner or a local show one evening a week. Unless he was working on his sermon, they usually spent part of Saturday together, too, sometimes visiting her grandmother, who was positively mad about his car.

"George, isn't that the young Reverend Talbot talking to the judge by the door over there?"

Abbie perked up visibly when she heard the woman in the next booth mention Seth sotto voce. She looked around, but she couldn't see him from where she was sitting.

"I think it is," the man in the next booth, obviously George, responded to the woman's low question.

"He isn't wearing his collar again," the woman said in disapproval, and Abbie hid a smile, reaching for the water glass. "His behavior isn't at all proper for a minister."

"You can't very well condemn the man just because he takes his collar off once in a while," George defended him carefully. "It's probably like wearing a tie. When I'm not working, I don't want one around my neck."

"It isn't only that, George," the woman insisted. "It's the way he's carrying on with that Scott girl."

Once she had started eavesdropping, it was impossible for Abbie to stop. She knew the gossip was running rampant because of the frequency of her dates with Seth. It was to be expected.

"Both of them are single. I don't see that there's anything wrong in him dating her," the man said. And Abbie thought, Hooray for George. At least he was sticking up for them against the malicious intonations of his wife, assuming the woman was his wife.

"She doesn't live with her parents, you know, although a lot of people think she does," the woman went on. "She fixed up an apartment for herself in the loft above the garage. It's completely private from the house." The woman's voice lowered to a conspiratorial whisper that Abbie was just barely able to catch. *"They say the reverend has been in her apartment."*

"Really." George's voice was dry with disinterest.

"Don't you think it's strange the way she came back so suddenly from Kansas City? Supposedly she gave up a good job." The remarks were full of malicious innuendos that had Abbie bristling. "If you ask me, there has to be a reason why someone as attractive as the Scott girl hasn't gotten married. I'll bet she's hiding something."

"You have a remarkable talent, Maude, for seeing sin in other people," George muttered.

"I still think he should be dating a nice girl instead. . . . Don't look now, George, but he's coming this way." In a louder voice, the woman issued a sweetly bright greeting. "Hello, Reverend. How are you today?"

"Fine, thank you," Seth's voice replied.

In the next second, he entered Abbie's side vision. She glanced at him briefly, her smile a little stiff. He slid onto the opposite booth seat, a warm light gleaming in his blue eyes for her.

"Hello, Abbie. You're early," he observed. "I thought I'd have to wait for you."

"I had a couple of errands to run." She opened her menu, willing herself not to pay any attention to the idle gossip she'd overheard.

But Seth was too well acquainted with her moods, too able to read her mind. "Is something wrong?" He tipped his head to one side, the thickness of his dark bronze hair showing signs of having been ruffled by the wind and then tamed with combing fingers.

Abbie started to deny that there was anything the matter, then she thought about the woman in the next booth, who must have realized she'd been sitting there all the time. When Abbie spoke, her voice was a little louder than it needed to be.

"I was just thinking about 'sticks and stones,'" she replied. Seth drew back, his gaze narrowing slightly to study her with a considering look. Abbie turned her attention on the menu, missing his glance at the booth behind her. "Meat loaf is the luncheon special today. It sounds good. I think that's what I'll have."

When the waitress came to take their order, Seth echoed her choice. "Might as well make it two luncheon specials." He waited until the waitress had left to ask, "How have you been?" As if it had been awhile since he'd seen her when it was only two days ago.

"Fine. By the way, I finished typing the manuscript," Abbie informed him. "It's safely delivered into the writers' hands already." Abbie was careful not to mention the Coltrain sisters by name, not with the possibility of a big set of ears listening.

"That's good timing," he replied.

It seemed a curious response. "Why is that?" She laughed shortly.

"Because I could use some help typing up some church notices I want to mail out next week. It shouldn't take you more than one evening."

"That sounds as if I've already volunteered," Abbie retorted in amusement.

"I knew you'd agree." Seth mockingly pretended she had. "Is there anything wrong with doing it tonight?"

"I suppose not," she replied, acknowledging that she would do it.

"Why don't you stop by the parsonage a little before seven?" he suggested. Abbie tensed, wondering what the woman in the next booth was making out of her going to the parsonage. "I have to be at the church shortly after seven for a wedding rehearsal," Seth added, and she breathed a silent sigh of relief. "You can have the office all to yourself. I wouldn't want to be accused of disturbing you while you were working."

"I should hope not. Shall I bring my typewriter or do you have one?" she asked.

"A manual."

"I'll bring my portable electric," Abbie stated.

Halfway through their lunch, a member of the church board stopped by the booth and sat down to chat a moment with Seth. Abbie heard the couple in the adjoining booth leave and relaxed a little.

Inevitably the conversation between Seth and the director turned to church matters, which fairly well left Abbie out of it. From church business, there was a natural transition to a

discussion of the Bible, and a pointed, but ami-
cable, difference of opinion about the correct
interpretation of a particular passage of the
Scriptures.

"You settle it, Miss Scott." The board member
turned to her for a third opinion. "What do you
think it means?"

She felt suddenly trapped, and embarrassed,
because she wasn't familiar with the passage
they were talking about at all. Seth came to her
rescue.

"I think Abbie is going to insist on remaining
neutral," he said. "She doesn't profess to be a
student of the Bible, so it isn't fair to ask her to
referee."

"The reverend is right." Abbie used his title
when referring to him in the company of others.
"I stay quietly neutral about such matters."

"I imagine you and the reverend have other
things to discuss besides the Bible." The man
winked.

It was an innocent remark, without any critical intention, yet Abbie wondered if she
shouldn't become more familiar with the Bible.
Just as this man had, others would expect her to
be more knowledgeable about it than she was.
The thought continued to prey at the back of her
mind through lunch, and the rest of the day as
well.

Abbie slowed the car as she neared the parsonage that evening. "I guess we might as well park
right out in front, Mabel. The whole town proba-

146

bly knows I'm going to be here tonight anyway," she murmured aloud to the car, and maneuvered the cranky vehicle close to the curb.

With the brake set, she stepped out of the car and walked around to the passenger side where her typewriter was sitting on the seat. The screen door to the parsonage banged shut. Abbie half turned to see Seth running lightly down the steps. He looked so striking, dressed all in black, with only the narrow band of his white collar for contrast.

"Let me carry that typewriter for you," he said as he approached the car.

"It's lightweight." Abbie objected to the notion that she needed any help, but he firmly took it out of her grasp.

"How would it look to the neighbors if I let you carry this into the house when I'm empty-handed?" Seth reasoned with a mocking gleam. "They'd think I didn't have any manners at all."

"And do you?" she challenged, and moved ahead of him to open the door, letting him enter the house first.

It was an old house with typically high ceilings. The screen door opened into a wide foyer with doors leading off from it. A throw rug didn't quite cover the worn patches of the carpet and layers of dark varnish covered the woodwork. The fern-patterned wallpaper probably had once matched the carpet on the floor but it had faded.

"The office is through here." Seth pushed open the door to the right with his foot.

Abbie followed him into the office. There was

an immediate difference. The entryway had created the overall impression of something tired and worn down, but the study had a vibrant warmth to it. A pair of plushly stuffed armchairs were covered in an ocher-gold corduroy, a color carried through in the drapes at the front window. The carpet was a pale cream shade that widened the paneled walls of the room.

"This is where you spend most of your time, isn't it?" Abbie guessed.

Seth placed the typewriter on his desk and turned to lean against the front side of the old walnut desk, letting his gaze sweep around the room before settling on Abbie. "It shows, does it?"

"Yes."

"I had the chairs recovered and bought new drapes and carpeting," he admitted. "The whole house needs something done to it, but I don't know what."

"It has a lot of possibilities."

"Such as?" Seth challenged dryly, and pushed away from the desk to walk to the middle of the room where she was standing.

"As old as this house is, I wouldn't be surprised if there are hardwood floors under that carpeting in the entryway. You could paint the walls a sunny yellow and brighten it up a lot," Abbie said, throwing out ideas off the top of her head.

"Would you like to fix the place up? I'll give you a free hand to do whatever you want," he offered.

It would be a challenge, but Abbie shook her head, expressing skepticism. "I don't think the church would go along with spending that much money on the parsonage. You'd have to go to the board with plans and estimates."

"The board wouldn't care if I paid for it out of my own pocket." Seth dismissed that obstacle. "What do you say? Do you want to do it?"

Again she shook her head. "People are talking now. Can you imagine their reaction if I started redecorating the parsonage?" Abbie eyed him as if he had taken complete leave of his senses.

"'Sticks and stones.'" He used her phrase from lunch that day—deliberately.

"'May break my bones.'" She continued the children's rhyme, but changed the ending to it. "But words can end up hurting you, Seth."

"And what about the words you heard today?" he challenged quietly.

"I don't know what you're talking about," Abbie protested.

"Yes, you do," he insisted, taking her by the arms and pulling her slowly toward him. "You overheard Mrs. Jones saying something before I arrived for lunch today, didn't you?"

"It was nothing. I just considered the source and forgot it. I'm not thin-skinned," she assured him, and spread her hands across the black material covering his chest.

"You have a very sensitive skin," Seth replied, and folded her into his arms to prove it, kissing her throat and the side of her neck.

Little quivers of delight ran along her flesh to

thrill her. His clean-shaven cheeks were smooth against her skin, the tangy fragrance of a male cologne stimulating her senses. It seemed every time he held her in his arms, she experienced this heady rapture that burned deep into her very soul.

"I thought you asked me here to type." The huskiness of her voice revealed how much he was disturbing her.

"Maybe I changed my mind." He burrowed his mouth into the side of her hair.

"What about the wedding rehearsal at the church?" she reminded him, then added to get his attention, "*Reverend*?"

"Now *that* was unkind." He lifted his head while his hands continued to glide up and down her back with lazy interest.

"The bride and groom can't practice without the minister." Her gaze lingered on the strong shape of his mouth, fascinated by the feelings it could evoke.

"But the minister isn't expected for another twenty minutes," Seth informed her. "That's plenty of time for Seth Talbot to—"

"Behave yourself, Seth." Her hands pushed against his chest as she suddenly realized the screen door was unlocked. Anyone could walk in and find them.

"Why?" He allowed her to create a small space between them, but kept his hands linked together behind her back. "Do you think I'm going to lose control of my prurient desires?"

"Don't you think you'd better show me what

you want typed?" Abbie suggested, unable to handle his conversation.

"I suppose." He sighed with mock reluctance. "Come on." He took her by the hand and led her to the desk where he'd set her typewriter. "Here are the envelopes." He pointed to a stack, then to a card file. "And in there are all the addresses of the names on the list."

"Is that it?" Abbie had been under the impression it was more complicated.

"That's it. Do you think you can handle it?" A light danced in his glittering blue eyes.

"It looks simple enough," she conceded. "Any schoolgirl with one semester of typing could do it."

Seth angled his body toward her, that disturbing darkness back in his look. "So you think you're overqualified for the task?" he challenged huskily.

"I didn't say that at all," Abbie denied with a reproving smile.

"Good, because there isn't anyone else I want to do it," Seth declared, then glanced at the wall clock with its swinging pendulum and sighed in regret. "It's time I was getting over to the church. Are you sure you don't have any questions?"

"None," she assured him.

"I don't know how long I'll be." He released her hand. "If anyone calls, they can reach me at the church."

"Okay." Abbie nodded.

His fingers gripped her chin to hold it still

while he pressed a warm kiss on her lips. Then he was drawing away, winking at her as he turned and walked to the door. In just that brief contact, her pulse beat at an irregular rhythm, affected by the possessive quality in his kiss.

The screen door banged shut before Abbie finally moved from where Seth had left her standing. She walked around the desk and found the outlet to plug her typewriter cord into, but her actions were all automatic, not directed by conscious thought. There had been nothing special in this parting, nothing to set it apart from others, yet Abbie had no more doubts about the way she felt toward him. Even without Seth there to disturb her senses and affect her physically, she was in love with him. The knowledge was clear and certain within her, no longer shadowed by question marks that it might be mere infatuation or physical attraction.

A small smile touched her lips as she sat down in his chair. There weren't any bells or lightning bolts, no blinding light—just the pure, warm feeling filling her whole being with the certainty of her emotion. It was a discovery to savor for the moment. Later on, she could wonder whether it was a love that was requited.

She rolled the first envelope into the typewriter and switched on the power, then went over the list of names and addresses to quickly familiarize herself with them before she started. Once she began, more time was spent taking the envelope in and out of the typewriter than typing.

A moth fluttered into the room, drawn to the goose-necked lamp that curved over the typewriter. Abbie let her fingers pause on the keys and arched her back muscles to ease their tension. With satisfaction, she noted that the stack of typed envelopes was taller than the stack of blank ones.

As she typed out the city and zip code to complete the address on the envelope in the carriage, the telephone rang. She picked up the receiver, using her shoulder to cradle it to her ear while she rolled the envelope from the typewriter.

"Parsonage." There was a faintly preoccupied tone to her voice. Silence followed on the other end of the line, drawing her full attention. She gripped the receiver in her hand and glanced at the mouth piece. "Hello?"

"Who is this?" a woman's voice sharply demanded.

"This is Miss Scott." Abbie identified herself, a defensiveness creeping into her words.

"I want to speak to Reverend Talbot. Is he there—with you?" The light emphasis on the last monosyllable made the woman's implication very plain.

"No, he isn't." Abbie made her voice very definite on that point. "Reverend Talbot had a wedding rehearsal this evening. You can reach him at the church."

"I have already tried the church, Miss Scott, and I didn't receive any answer," was the haughty reply. "Are you sure Reverend Talbot isn't there?" The question blatantly implied that Abbie was lying.

"I am very sure," Abbie retorted, just managing to keep her temper. "Perhaps you should try phoning the church again and letting it ring. It's possible Reverend Talbot wasn't able to answer it earlier."

"And it's possible he isn't there," the woman responded. "Do you have any idea what time it is, Miss Scott?"

She had been so busy typing that she hadn't paid any attention to the hour, except to note that it had grown dark outside. She glanced at the wall clock, a little surprised to learn how much time had gone by. "It's eighteen minutes after nine."

"Would you mind telling me what you're doing at the parsonage at this hour, Miss Scott?" the woman challenged.

"The reverend had some typing that needed to be done." If it weren't for the possibility that Seth might suffer the repercussions of her rudeness, Abbie would have informed the woman that it was none of her business.

"How convenient," the woman murmured dryly.

"If the reverend comes back in the next few minutes, may I tell him who called?" Abbie sweetly demanded to know the woman's identity.

But the woman ignored the question. "I'll do as you suggested, Miss Scott, and try the church again." There was a click as the connection was broken, followed by the hum of the dial tone.

Burning with indignant anger, Abbie slammed the receiver down. Her lips were pressed tightly together as she glanced at the window. She hoped the woman had to eat all her nasty little thoughts when Seth answered the phone at the church. A flicker of curiosity ran through her mind and she wondered why he hadn't answered when the woman had supposedly rang the church earlier.

The question impelled her to leave the desk and cross the room to the front window. The outer darkness created mirrorlike reflections in the glass panes, making it difficult for Abbie to see outside. There didn't appear to be any lights burning in the church. A frown narrowed her eyes. If the wedding rehearsal was over, where was Seth? Bewildered, she turned from the window and walked blindly back to the desk. She had to force herself to concentrate on typing the balance of the envelopes.

Forty-five minutes later, she took the last one out of the typewriter. A dull pain was pounding at her temples. She rubbed at it with her fingertips, but it didn't go away. Sighing heavily, Abbie turned in the chair to arrange the typed envelopes in neat stacks. The desk lamp cast a pool of light over her work area but shadows lurked in the rest of the office-study.

"All finished?"

The voice from the shadows made Abbie

jump. She hadn't heard Seth come in. His black-clad form blended with the darkened opening of the entryway. He was leaning a shoulder against the door frame, arms crossed, when she saw him. She had the impression he'd been watching her for some time.

"I didn't hear you come in," Abbie declared after the shock of discovering she wasn't alone had passed.

"Sorry." Seth pushed away from the door, unfolding his arms to lower them to his side as he walked to the desk and into the pool of light. There was something deeply disturbing about the way he was looking at her. Her heart seemed to do crazy, little flip-flops. "I didn't mean to startle you."

"It's all right. Did you just come from the church? I thought it looked dark when I glanced outside earlier," Abbie said.

He sat sideways on the front of the desk, an amused glint in his blue eyes as he surveyed her. "Checking up on me, were you?" Seth chided dryly.

Abbie hadn't meant to give him that impression and rushed to explain. "No, it's just that a woman called here for you and said she hadn't received any answer when she rang the church. I suggested she try again and let it ring. Did you talk to her?"

"No." An absent frown crossed his rugged features. "What time was it?"

"Almost twenty minutes after nine."

"I'd already left the church by then," Seth

admitted, then noticed the questioning look that flickered uncertainly in Abbie's glance. An amused line lifted the edges of his strong mouth. "The groom's parents had a late buffet supper at their house for the wedding party, which I was expected to attend. I put in a brief appearance and left," he explained. "Did the woman leave her name or a message?"

"No. When she didn't call back, I assumed she had probably reached you at the church." Since Seth hadn't been there, Abbie could easily guess what the woman had conjectured from that. She didn't mention the snide comments the woman had made to her.

"Whatever she wanted to speak to me about couldn't have been too important, or she would have called back," Seth concluded, dismissing the matter from the conversation. "Since you're all finished with the typing, how about some coffee?"

If it hadn't been for the woman's phone call, Abbie probably would have accepted the offer. But she was conscious of being alone with him in the parsonage. "It's awfully late. I'd better not." She refused with a shake of her pale auburn hair and leaned down to unplug her typewriter. It was already after ten o'clock, and someone was bound to notice her car was still parked outside.

"In that case . . ." Seth straightened from the desktop when Abbie stood up to wind the cord around the typewriter. ". . . I'll just have to come up with some other reason to persuade you to stay." He moved leisurely around the desk to come up behind her.

"Seth," she protested self-consciously as he slid his hands around to the front of her waist to pull her back against him.

Her entire back was molded to the unmistakable maleness of his solid chest, flat muscled stomach, and thrusting hips. Abbie made a token attempt to push aside the hands circling her rib cage and stopping tantalizingly near the straining swell of her breasts. But she signaled the weakness of her opposition by tilting her head to the side to give his nuzzling mouth access to the bare curve of her neck.

A rising heat flooded through her veins to melt her into pliancy while he nibbled along the sensitive cord near the base of her shoulder. Her eyes drifted closed under the waves of excited sensation. His arms tightened around her, one hand sliding lower onto her stomach and igniting another kind of ache.

The ringing of the telephone was a decidedly unwelcome intrusion, but definitely a timely one, or Abbie might have yielded to Seth's delaying tactics. She felt him stiffen in resistance to the telephone's summons.

Drawing a shaky breath, she insisted, "You'd better answer that."

"I know," he muttered, and reluctantly let her out of his embrace to step toward the desk and pick up the phone. "Reverend Talbot speaking."

Immediately Abbie took advantage of his distraction to lift her portable typewriter into her arms. If she didn't leave now, chances were that it would be much later before she did. Seth sliced her an impatient look when he realized her intention.

"Just a minute," he said to the caller, and lowered the receiver to cover the mouthpiece with his hand. "Abbie, you don't have to leave."

"Yes, I do," she insisted, and moved out of his reach, walking toward the entryway and the front door. "It's late and I have to work tomorrow."

"Abbie—"

"Is that the woman who phoned earlier?" She paused in the shadowed doorway.

"Yes, I think it is but—" It was of no consequence to him; that much was clear in his expression.

"You'd better not keep her waiting," Abbie advised, because it would probably just fuel the woman's imagination. "Bye."

Without waiting for him to respond in kind, Abbie left the office-study and walked with quick, purposeful strides to the screen door. She pushed it open with the side of her arm, her hands carrying the typewriter. As she stepped outside she heard Seth talking on the phone again.

Chapter Nine

A steady rain beat against the panes of her apartment windows. Gray, dismal clouds cast a depressing gloom into the living area. Abbie wandered restlessly from the window and the rain that showed no signs of letting up. She was at a loss for something to do.

There was nothing interesting on television and the radio offered no less passive entertainment. She paused in front of the low shelf of books and glanced over the titles. One seemed to jump out at her, its gold lettering gleaming against its maroon background—Holy Bible. It was the Revised Standard Version of the King James Bible, a gift from the church when she had become a member.

After a brief second's consideration, Abbie slipped it from the shelf and carried it over to the sofa. She curled herself on one corner of the couch with her legs tucked under her and began leafing through the pages. There was a vague thought at the back of her mind that she might accidentally run across the passage Seth had been discussing at lunch the other day.

Since Seth was a minister, the chances were good that there would be more conversations like that one, and her ignorance of the Bible would only become more noticeable. It was something she needed to correct.

A noise made itself heard above the steady patter of rain on the roof. Abbie lifted her head to listen, but she didn't hear anything more. She flipped through a few more pages, then stopped, out of loyalty to her sex, to read the Book of Ruth in the Old Testament. Halfway down the first column, she heard footsteps on the stairs.

The knowledge ran swift and sure within her that it had to be Seth. Even though there hadn't been any definite arrangement for him to see her this Saturday, she had guessed he would come by or call if he was free. She swung her feet to the floor, leaving the Bible lying open on the cushion beside her, and hurried to the door.

There was a knock just before she reached it. Abbie opened the door to see Seth standing outside, rainwater dripping from his jacket. He was wiping the wetness from his face, then shaking it from his hand.

"It's raining," he offered wryly.

"I never would have guessed." Abbie laughed and opened the door wider to let him in. "I'll get you a towel." She walked to the kitchen area to fetch him a hand towel from a cupboard drawer. "Don't you have an umbrella, or did you forget to put the top up on your car?"

"An umbrella, that's what I forgot," Seth mocked as he shrugged out of his jacket.

The rainy autumn weather had brought a damp chill to the air. Abbie noticed Seth was wearing an ivory pullover in a wide-ribbed knit as a concession to the cooler temperatures. It emphasized the width of his shoulders and the solidness of his muscular chest, tapering as it did to his narrow waist and hips. The rain had darkened his hair to a bronze brown, gleaming in the apartment's artificial light.

"Do you have any plans for this afternoon?" he asked when she returned with the towel, giving it to him and taking his jacket.

"Nothing. As a matter of fact I was becoming bored with my own company." She hooked his jacket on an arm of the wooden clothes tree by the door. "Why? Where were you thinking of going?"

"I wasn't thinking of going anywhere, but right here," Seth replied. When Abbie turned to look uncertainly at him, he looped the towel around her neck and held both ends to pull her toward him. There was a heady excitement in the lazy way he looked at her.

"And do what?" she asked, not really meaning to sound provocative.

Bending his head, Seth kissed at her lips. Weak-limbed, Abbie clutched at his forearms for support. "What were you doing when I came?" he murmured between kisses, the heated warmth of his breath mingling with hers. "Whatever it was, that's what we can do—

among other things, like this." His mouth closed onto her lips, finally giving her a chance to respond. When he lifted his head, Abbie was contentedly lost in a glorious daze. "Aren't you going to invite me to sit down?" he chided.

"Have a seat." Her hand moved through the air to obligingly second the invitation.

He released one end of the towel and swept it from around her neck, then took her hand to bring her with him as he walked to the sofa. The opened Bible occupied the middle cushion. Seth picked it up to move it so they could sit together, then recognized the holy book. He cocked a curious look at Abbie.

"What's this?" he asked, and glanced at the book it was opened to. "You were reading the Book of Ruth?"

A smile teased her mouth as she remembered his earlier question. "That's what I was doing when you came."

"Any particular reason?" An eyebrow was lifted with speculating interest. "Or are you just trying to impress me?" He sat down on the middle cushion while Abbie bent a knee under her to sit on the end.

"Since I didn't know you were coming, I can't be guilty of trying to impress you," she denied, aware his question had been only half-serious. "I admit I was slightly prejudiced when I picked out the Book of Ruth to read, since it's about a woman. It seemed to be the fair thing to do, to stick up for my sex."

"It's a very logical choice," Seth agreed, leaning against the back rest. "I apologize if I was wrong the other day at lunch when I indicated you weren't well enough acquainted with the Scriptures to offer an opinion."

"You don't need to apologize, because you were right," Abbie admitted with a rueful shrug. "That's why I picked it up to read and learn more about what's in it than the stories they taught me in Sunday school."

"I see," he murmured, absently looking at the opened pages.

"It's a shame there isn't anyone around who could tutor me." She sighed in mock regret, a teasing sparkle in her glance.

"Is that a broad hint that you want to spend the afternoon with me—reading the Bible?" Seth countered with a glittering look that lingered on her mouth, made softer by his kisses.

"You were the one who suggested we could spend the afternoon doing whatever I was doing when you arrived," Abbie reminded him with a small, dimpling smile.

"So I did." His smile was turned down at the corners but no less filled with amusement. "And ministers don't lie, so I guess I'll have to read to you from the Bible." He began turning pages. "Do you have any requests?"

"No." Abbie shook her head. "You choose."

"Let's see." Seth paused, partially closing the book to skip ahead. "What would you like to hear?" It was a rhetorical question, absently murmured aloud. "Something for Abbie. Abra, the namesake of Solomon's favorite. The Song of Solomon." He reopened the Bible to that book of the Old Testament and arched her a glance. "Does that sound appropriate?"

"Very," she agreed, and turned to lean against the sofa's armrest, facing him more squarely.

She watched him turn a couple of pages as if selecting a particular passage, then stop when he found what he was looking for. There was something vaguely enigmatic in the glance that ran over her face.

"From the Song of Solomon," Seth repeated, and began reading in a voice that was vibrant with expression and pitched low.

"How fair and pleasant you are,
    O loved one, delectable maiden!"

The words seemed to send a caressing finger down her spine. It was not what she had expected to hear. The beat of her pulse picked up a little in anticipation, her gaze locking onto his face and watching his mouth form the words when he continued.

"You are stately as a palm tree,
    And your breasts are like its clusters.
I say I will climb the palm tree
    And lay hold of its branches."

Her breathing stopped at the passion and promise in his low voice. A fiery warmth burned through her veins, heating her skin with the things he was saying—the boldness of them, and the beauty of them.

> "Oh, may your breasts be like clusters of
>   the vine,
> And the scent of your breath like
>   apples,
> And your kisses like the best wine
>   that goes down smoothly,
> Gliding over lips and teeth."

Seth lifted his gaze from the pages, his deeply blue eyes turning their attention to her. Abbie was helpless to conceal how much the passionate selection had affected her. She was trembling with the desire it had aroused.

Taking the book, he turned it and offered it to her. "Now, it's your turn to read to me." She took it with both hands and glanced dazedly at the page. "Start from here." His fingers pointed out where she was to begin.

Her voice had a husky sound as Abbie began reading the words, and feeling them, too.

> "I am my beloved's,
>   and his desire is for me
> Come, my beloved,
>   let us go forth into the fields,
>   and lodge in the villages;
> Let us go out early to the vineyards,
>   and see whether the vines have
>   budded,

Whether the grape blossoms have
  opened
And the pomegranates are in
  bloom.
There . . ."

Abbie paused, her voice dropping to a whisper
as she lifted her gaze to Seth. "'. . . I will give
you my love.'"

"Will you?" he murmured and leaned toward
her.

"Yes," she whispered with an aching need to
give to him, seduced by her own undeniable love
for him.

She didn't know he took the Bible from her
hands and laid it aside. She seemed not to be
aware of anything but the pounding of her own
heart and the deeply blue eyes that held her
forever captivated by their fire.

"Then come here, my delectable maiden."
His hands closed firmly on her waist, near her
hipbones, and impelled her to slide toward
him.

Like a willow, she bent under the leaning
force of his body. His mouth was mere inches
from hers as he gently lowered her to the sofa,
the weight of his hard body pressed alongside
hers. It was a moment lost in time, without a
beginning or an end.

It could have been seconds or minutes before
Abbie felt the warmth of his mouth on her lips. It
was a kiss of raw wonder that searched and
explored the boundless limits of pleasure, then

deepened with the insatiable hunger that grew more intense with each taste. Her lips parted under the hungry probe of his tongue to know more of her. Abbie trembled at the fullness that came with the exchange, and the appetite it aroused for still more.

Her legs were tangled with his as her hands roamed over his sweater-covered shoulders, feeling his muscles flex and ripple beneath the ribbed knit material. His mouth rolled over her parted lips while his tongue lightly traced the sensitive inside corners, drawing a moan from her throat.

"Your kisses are like wine, Abra," Seth murmured into her mouth. "Intoxicating and smooth, 'gliding over lips and teeth.'"

And he drank of them again, but Abbie was certain she was the one who was drunk with love for him. It was a shattering experience to be helpless with longing, desperately needing what another person had to give. She strained closer to the raw heat of his body, hard and aroused against her side. His mouth was on her lips, her throat, her ear, her neck, wildly delighting her wherever it touched and tasted.

His fingers were on the buttons of her blouse, deftly slipping them free from the stitched holes, surely working their way downward. Briefly her flesh was exposed to the coolness of the air until his hand warmed it, spreading his heat and making it hers.

Then his head was turning to look at the

feminine beauty he had exposed. Abbie felt no need to conceal her body from his gaze. She loved him and his desire was for her. She wanted him to be pleased with her—with all and everything that made her unique.

"You have lovely breasts, Abra," he declared thickly. "Lovely."

His hand cupped a creamy breast in his palm; his stroking fingers evoked an intimate pleasure so intense it was like pain. His mouth came down to ease the ache and make its own tactile exploration of the hills and valleys and hardened peaks of her breasts. She was a tightly coiled spring inside, wanting to absorb him into her flesh and needing the absolute closeness of love's consummation.

"Love me, Seth," she whispered, her fingers curling into the faint dampness of his hair. It was less a request for physical possession and more a prayer for emotional commitment—that it be as beautiful and meaningful to him as it was to her.

He dragged his mouth roughly across the hollow of her throat, a groan coming from deep inside him. "Abbie, don't ask that of me," he protested.

"But—" The sharp ache of rejection choked her voice, stabbing her with remorse.

"It can't be," he insisted with a trace of hard-jawed anger. "Not for you and me."

His hands pulled her blouse closed, firmly crossing the material. Then he gathered her hard into his arms, flattening her breasts against his chest and burying his face in her hair. The tautness of his long body was pressed into hers, making its male angles intimately felt. It was almost torture to have him so close and know there would be no satisfaction. Abbie wasn't sure why. Her thoughts were too muddled with unfulfilled desires to make anything clear. She clung to him.

"Abbie." Seth released her name in the middle of a long, heavy sigh. "I want you. I'm not pretending to deny that."

"Neither am I," she murmured rawly.

A sound, something like weary laughter, came from him. "What am I going to do with you, Abbie?" The rhetorical question he muttered only confused her more.

The telephone, positioned on the table at the end of the sofa, rang shrilly, almost in her ear. Abbie stiffened with a guilty start, as if the caller could see them locked so intimately in a prone position. There was a moment of indecision while she debated whether to answer it or let it ring. Seth took the decision from her, loosening his arms to let her go.

"You'd better answer it," he advised with husky reluctance. "It could be important."

She moved away from him to sit up shakily, partially turning her back to him. On the fifth ring, she picked up the receiver while the fingers of her free hand fumbled with buttons on her blouse.

"Hello." She heard the breathlessness in her

voice, caused not from exertion but from the softness of love.

"Miss Scott?" a woman's voice demanded.

An icy chill ran down her spine as Abbie recognized the voice as belonging to the same woman who had called the parsonage the other night.

"Yes." She was stiff and wary. "Who is this?"

"This is Mrs. Cones. I'm trying to locate Reverend Talbot. Is he there? It's urgent that I talk to him," the woman stated.

Abbie pressed the receiver to her chest and glanced over her shoulder. Seth was sitting and raking a hand through his hair. "It's a Mrs. Cones," Abbie whispered. "She wants to talk to you."

His head lifted, as if scenting trouble, then a blandness stole over his features as he reached out a hand to take the phone. "I'll talk to her."

"Just a moment," Abbie said into the phone.

"He's there? I thought as much." The woman sniffed in a haughty way.

A scorching heat burned her cheeks at the accuracy of the woman's vile imagination. Abbie avoided looking at Seth as she rose from that end of the sofa and handed him the phone. She moved to the center of the room using both hands to button the rest of her blouse and smooth the dishevelment of her clothes.

"This is Reverend Talbot speaking," she heard Seth say into the phone.

Not wanting to hear even one side of the conversation, Abbie walked to the window to stare at the falling rain. She rested a hot cheek against the coolness of a glass pane and blanked everything from her mind.

When Seth's hand touched her shoulder, she was brought back to a world of awareness. There was a slight movement of her head to acknowledge his presence, but she didn't turn from the window.

"I'm sorry that happened, Abbie," he said.

"It's all right." But the words made her hurt inside, and it was evident in the flatness of her voice.

"Wait a minute." His fingers dug impatiently into her shoulder and forced her to turn at right angles to the window and partially face him. "I'm apologizing for the phone call—not for anything else." Although her expression changed little, the dull green flecks in her hazel eyes brightened visibly. His gaze narrowed on them in satisfaction. "Not for anything else," Seth repeated for emphasis.

"I'm sorry about that phone call, too," Abbie admitted, because it seemed the safest comment to make. There didn't seem to be any point to reiterating her feelings for him. She had already expressed them very explicitly, both by word and deed.

The hand on her shoulder eased its pressure but continued to hold her. "Do you want to know why I chose that particular section from the Bible?"

"Why?" Perhaps his answer would tell her what she wanted to hear.

"Because I wanted you to see it's a book of love and passion, suffering and caring, but mainly it's a book of love," he explained. It was a subject she was intimately familiar with, since its richness filled her. "Don't look at me like that, Abbie." A muscle leaped along his jaw, revealing an inner strain for control.

"Like what?" It seemed no different to Abbie than the way she'd always looked at him.

"Like—" His mouth came down to crush her lips in a fiercely possessive kiss. It took her breath and made a mockery of her normal heartbeat. When he pulled away, his mouth was edged with tautness and his blue eyes glittered with turbulence. His voice fell somewhere between a groan and a curse. "I'm made of flesh the same as you are, Abbie."

"I think I've always known that," Abbie admitted as she leaned back against the coolness of the window to study him. "I just kept letting the collar get in the way."

"You think I haven't known that," Seth murmured dryly, including a slight shake of his head with the reply. His hand moved over her shoulder in a restless caress. "There's a lot we need to talk about, Abbie, but I don't have time now. Mrs. Cones called because her mother is in the hospital, very ill, and her father—the woman's husband—is overwrought. I promised I'd come sit with him for a while so I have to leave."

"I understand," Abbie assured him, smothering her regret that he had to go now.

"Will you wait for me after church tomorrow?

We'll have Sunday dinner together here or at the parsonage. It doesn't matter, just as long as we can have the privacy to talk," he said.

"I don't think the parsonage is a good idea." Neither place was exactly wise but Abbie suggested, "Why don't we eat here? I can put a roast in the oven so dinner can be ready when church is over."

"That's fine." His glance flicked past her to the falling rain outside, then returned to sweep her face. There seemed to be struggle going on inside him. "I have to leave now," Seth stated with grim determination, and kissed her hard before turning away to walk swiftly to the door, as if he thought he might change his mind.

He grabbed his jacket from the hall tree and opened the door, pausing to look over his shoulder at Abbie standing by the window. His mouth twitched with a quick, hard smile, then he was walking out the door, pulling it closed behind him.

Chapter Ten

Abbie followed the line of people shaking hands with Seth as they left the church. When it was her turn, she placed her hand in his and felt his grip tighten in firm possession. There was an added vibrancy in his blue eyes, an interest meant for her alone.

"Good morning, Miss Scott." He faintly drawled the words, as if mocking the formality.

"Good morning, Reverend," she echoed his greeting, a responding smile playing with the corners of her mouth. Abbie was conscious of others listening to their exchange, some critically and some with simple curiosity.

"Your parents aren't with you?" Seth observed with a questioning inflection in his voice.

"No. They went out of town today—to Missouri to visit some friends," she explained.

"I hope you've fixed a good Sunday dinner then."

"I have," Abbie assured him, fully aware that

his comment was a subtle reminder they would be sharing it together. It was written in the way he was looking at her.

Then he was releasing her hand to greet the next ones in line and Abbie moved on. At the base of the steps, she angled to the edge of the sidewalk, removing herself from the flow of people leaving the church. She lingered there to wait for Seth.

The Coltrain sisters spied her as they came down the steps in a glaring mismatch of colors— Isabel dressed in pink and Esther in bright orange. The two sisters were inseparable, yet they seemed determined to establish their own individualities, hence their clashing clothes. Abbie smiled a greeting as the pair converged on her.

"Good morning," she said, noting the excitement in their faces.

"We saw you in church and we were hoping we'd have a chance to speak to you," Isabel rushed.

"Yes." Esther echoed her sister's words and leaned closer to Abbie to whisper conspiratorially, "We mailed the you-know-what to a company in New York."

"The reverend gave us the man's name. He'd already talked to him personally about us and the man wanted to see—what we'd done. Isn't that wonderful?" Isabel nearly giggled like a giddy young girl.

"It certainly is." Abbie didn't have to pretend to be happy for them. She was hardly a judge but she had enjoyed the novel they'd written and felt certain a publisher would like it, too.

"The reverend said it might take two months before we hear what the man thought about—it," Esther explained. "But . . ." She hesitated and glanced at her sister.

"Esther and I have another idea," Isabel spoke up. "But we aren't sure whether we should start on it until we've found out about the first. We could just be wasting our time."

"Yes, and we wanted to ask you what you thought we should do," Esther finished.

"If it were me, I'd go ahead and start working on it," Abbie replied, and their faces lit up.

"Do you hear that Esther?" Isabel declared. "I just knew she'd say that. Didn't I tell you?"

"If we didn't have you and the reverend to talk to about this, I think Isabel and I would bust," Esther insisted, ignoring the "I-told-you-so" challenge from her sister.

"You'll do the typing on this one for us, won't you?" Isabel inquired anxiously.

"Of course, I will." She could hardly refuse.

"You really are a wonderful girl," Esther said, and squeezed Abbie's hand. "And you shouldn't pay any attention to all that talk going around. Those people spreading it are just nasty busybodies who don't have anything better to do." She didn't appear to notice the sudden tension that whitened Abbie's face as she turned to her sister. "We have to get home, Isabel."

"Yes. Now that you've agreed that it's the right thing to do to start on another one, we have a lot of research we need to begin. We don't mean to rush off," Isabel explained. "But you do understand."

"Of course." But it was a somewhat absent response Abbie gave as the two women hurried away.

Abbie had known her relationship with Seth had stirred up a lot of idle gossip. It was to be expected when a local minister was involved. Some of the remarks that had gotten back to her had been unfair and unkind. She had always been more concerned about all the talk affecting Seth's standing in the community rather than her own. But Esther's comment seemed to indicate Abbie was the one being maligned, and she was absolutely helpless to do anything about it. It did little good to tell herself she shouldn't be bothered by vicious gossip, because she suddenly was.

The stream of people coming out of church had ended, although the doors remained open. There was no sign of Seth, but Abbie assumed he had gone to change out of his robes. The church grounds and parking lot were virtually emptied of people and cars. She felt rather conspicuous standing near the bottom of the church steps and decided it would be more discreet if she waited inside the door.

As she entered the church she heard voices coming from the pulpit area. She recognized Seth's among them and was drawn across the small entry area by an inner need to see him. Seth and three other men were standing by the front pew. Abbie noticed he was still wearing his black robe. She had no intention of intruding or even eavesdropping. The three men were members of the governing board, so Seth was obviously discussing some church business with them.

Before she could turn away to wait near the front doors, she heard one of the men mention her name. She was held motionless, frozen by a kind of dread. Against her will, Abbie listened to what they were saying.

"We don't mean to sound critical, Reverend." A bald-headed man was speaking in a stiffly censorious voice that belied his words. "But we have an obligation to ourselves and the church to express our feelings on this matter."

"I'm sure your intentions are above reproach." Seth's murmured response was exceedingly dry. Even from this distance, Abbie could see the coldness in his blue eyes and the attitude of challenge in his stance.

"It isn't that we have anything personal against Miss Scott." A second man hurried to assure Seth of that.

"We freely acknowledge that she comes from a good family. Her parents are respected members of the community and this church," the third man said. "Miss Scott herself is probably a very nice girl."

"However?" Seth prompted the qualification that had only been implied by their tones.

"However . . ." The bald-headed man glanced at his two colleagues. ". . . she doesn't strike us as being a suitable . . . companion"—he paused before selecting the words—"for the minister of our church."

"Since Miss Scott has returned to our town, she hasn't participated actively in church affairs. She didn't even attend church on a frequent basis until you came," the third man explained.

"These are things you couldn't have known about her," the second man inserted. "Which was why we felt we should bring it to your attention."

"I'm sure you understand now why we are advising you to break off your relationship with Miss Scott. It would be in the best interest of everyone concerned," the bald-headed man concluded, with a slightly righteous tilt of his head.

Tears burned the back of her eyes as Abbie heard the final edict. She hadn't dreamed that anything like this might happen. The whole scene took on a nightmarish unreality. Her gaze clung to Seth as the silence stretched over the span of several seconds.

"I fully understand the concern that prompted you to seek me out, so this could be discussed openly." Seth's low-pitched voice was clear and concise. "And I'm in full agreement with you that Miss Scott lacks some of the qualifications that are regarded as essential for a woman to be considered as a minister's marital partner. . . ."

An involuntary gasp of pain was ripped from her throat at this ultimate condemnation from the man she loved. Abbie cupped a hand to her mouth to smother any more sounds, but it was already too late. Seth had seen her.

"Abbie!" He called to her.

But she heard the irritation in his voice and whirled away to run out the door. Tears blurred her vision as she hurried down the steps, breathing in sobs. Her high-heeled shoes restricted her pace to a running walk.

All her illusions were torn asunder. She suddenly realized why Seth had wanted to talk privately to her today. He had intended to break it to her gently that she wouldn't be a suitable wife for him. Love had led her down another dead-end road.

Yesterday, that passionate scene on her apartment sofa had been just that—passion—at least on Seth's part. Now Abbie could see what he had been trying to tell her when he had asserted he was made of flesh. The desires of the flesh—as opposed to the desires of the heart.

She remembered the way he had held her and murmured, "What am I going to do with you, Abbie?" Tears ran hotly down her cheeks as she reached her car in the church lot. It was all very clear now why he had said that. No doubt Seth had guessed that she was in love with him, but marriage was out of the question. What a fool she'd been! What an unmitigated fool!

"Abbie!"

Her glance was jerked in the direction of Seth's voice. He was half running across the lawn toward her, his black robe billowing out behind him. The flutterings of panic went through her. She couldn't face him, not yet—maybe never.

Wiping at the tears running down her cheeks, Abbie yanked open the car door and scrambled behind the wheel. Her shaking hands dived into her purse for the key and fumbled in their first attempt to insert it into the ignition lock. She glanced frantically out the front windshield. Seth was nearly to the car, a forbidding grimness etched into his rugged features.

"Don't fail me now, Mabel," Abbie pleaded with the car as she turned the key in the switch.

The motor grumbled in protest but its slowly turning noises were encouraging. Abbie pumped on the pedal to give it more gas and the grumble became a constant complaint. The gears ground together as she shifted into reverse, but it was too late.

Seth was opening the passenger door and reaching across the seat. Abbie pressed herself against the driver's door to elude him, but he wasn't intending to grab her. He was after the key. By the time she realized it, he had already turned the motor off and extracted the key from the ignition.

Cornered, Abbie squared around to face the front and gripped the steering wheel with both hands. She held herself rigid, refusing to look at him, not wanting to see the pity in his eyes.

"Will you please give me the keys?" she requested stiffly. Her jaw was white with the effort to contain her emotional turmoil.

There was a rustle of material as Seth climbed

into the passenger side and shut the door. Tension screamed through her nerves when he leaned over and inserted the key into the ignition switch.

"There's your key," he challenged.

Her chin started to quiver. Abbie had to grit her teeth to control it. "Will you please get out of my car?" she insisted, still without looking at him.

"We're having Sunday dinner together, remember?" Seth replied evenly.

"The invitation is withdrawn," Abbie retorted wildly, and blinked quickly to keep back the tears.

"That's too bad. I guess I'll just have to sit and watch you eat," he countered. "But we're going to get this misunderstanding straightened out."

"There is nothing to straighten out." She lifted her chin a little higher. "The situation has been made perfectly clear to me, so we have nothing to discuss. I understand completely."

"Do you?" he murmured dryly.

"Yes, I do," Abbie stated. "There's nothing you have to explain."

"Whether you want me to or not, I'm going to do just that," he stated. "You obviously overheard my meeting with the representatives from the church board."

"Obviously," she admitted on a bitter note, and flashed him a brief glance that was almost her undoing. The brooding intensity of his gaze seemed to reach out for her, but she succeeded in avoiding it.

"There are a great many disadvantages to marrying a minister. Your weekends are never free. Come rain, shine, sleet, or hail, you're in church on Sunday mornings. A lot of week-nights, your husband is gone attending church meetings. Everything you do is scrutinized by the good members of the congregation, from the clothes you wear to the way you fix your hair. You're expected to join every charity, every social and church group, and attend every meeting, unless your children are sick. You—"

"Stop it!" Abbie closed her eyes, unable to take anymore. "I'm fully aware I don't qualify for the position, so you don't have to give me a bunch of reasons why I wouldn't want it anyway!"

"You may not be applying for the position, Abbie," Seth said quietly, "but I'm asking you to fill it."

She caught her breath at his words, but refused to believe he meant them. Her eyes were bright with tears when she finally opened them and turned an accusing glance at him. "I heard what you said in there, Seth," she reminded him. "I don't—"

"If you had stayed to hear what else I had to say . . ." Seth interrupted, ". . . you would know I don't care whether you'd make a suitable minister's wife or not. You're the woman I want to marry."

"I . . ." Abbie stared at him incredulously, daring to listen. "Is this a proposal?"

"Yes." A slow smile began to spread across his mouth. "I'd get down on one knee but Mabel has me in cramped quarters." He hitched up his robe to reach in his pants pocket. "I was going to offer you this after dinner."

Dazed, Abbie slowly uncurled her fingers from their death grip on the steering wheel as she caught the sparkle of a diamond ring. When he reached out for her hand, she hesitantly offered him her left. She watched him slip the ring onto her third finger. "It's beautiful," she murmured.

"Does that mean you'll marry me?" Seth mocked.

"Yes . . . if you're sure." Abbie qualified her acceptance.

"I am very sure," he insisted, and proceeded to prove it.

His kiss was ardently possessive and demanding as his arm circled her waist to pull her across the seat to achieve a more satisfactory closeness. There was a wild singing in her ears, a rush of joy that was almost unbearably sweet. When he finally dragged his mouth from hers, she buried her face in the silklike robe covering his chest.

"I never realized I could be so happy." Abbie breathed out the words. "I thought I'd lost you."

"Not a chance." His fingers tunneled into her auburn hair and lifted her head so he could study her love-softened features. "You are going to be my wife . . . Mrs. Seth Talbot."

Hearing it made her tremble with happiness. "I still can't believe that you want to marry me, but I'm glad you do."

"Don't you remember the second time we met,

I told your mother that I hadn't married because I hadn't found anyone who was suitable for me," Seth reminded her. "I was never looking for a suitable minister's wife. I wanted a woman who would be right for me. You are that woman, Abbie."

"I had forgotten you had said that," she admitted.

"Maybe if you had remembered, you wouldn't have run out of the church the way you did." His mouth twisted in a wry line. "If you only knew how frightened I was at that moment—and how angry I was, too, because their unthinking remarks had hurt you."

"It wasn't just what they said, but the remarks *you* made yesterday, too," Abbie explained.

"The remarks I made?" He quirked an eyebrow. "What did I say to give you the wrong impression?"

"It was a lot of little things. When I wanted you to love me, you refused and told me not to ask that of you," she remembered.

"That's simply because I didn't want to anticipate our wedding night," Seth explained, then shook his head in stunned disbelief. "I suppose you thought I was saying that I couldn't love you."

"Not at that moment, I didn't think it—only later when I began piecing things together," Abbie admitted ruefully, because she had gotten the picture all wrong.

"What things?"

"Like when you said you didn't know what you

were going to do with me, I thought you were trying to find a way to break it to me gently that you didn't love me."

"I love you," Seth stated, so there would be no more question of that. "As for that remark, I'm not really sure what I meant other than that I'd been waiting for so long for you to finally recognize I was a man, that I loved you as a man. Because I was a minister you kept trying to put me above such things. Yesterday you nearly made me forget I was a minister, too."

"And I'll learn to be a good minister's wife," Abbie said, tracing her fingers along his jaw and trailing them across the slashing groove to the corner of his mouth.

"That's the other thing I was trying to explain to you yesterday. I don't want you to feel that because of me, it's your duty to know the Bible, or attend church, or anything else. If you want to do it, then let it be for the same reason I have. Do it for the love of God, not because you feel obligated because you are the minister's wife."

"I will," she whispered. "I promise you that."

His arms tightened around her, gathering her against him as his mouth came down to claim her lips. It was a long and passionate kiss that rocked Abbie all the way to her toes. She felt him shudder and bury his mouth in her hair.

"How I love you, Abbie," he muttered thickly.

"Seth." When she opened her eyes, her glance strayed over his shoulder to the walls of the church. "Do you realize we are practically necking in the church parking lot?"

A low chuckle came from him after a second's stillness. He lifted his head, amusement crinkling the corners of his eyes. "Can you think of a better place? I love you. In the eyes of God and the eyes of man, I want you for my wife."

"And I want you for my husband," she whispered, because she couldn't think of a better place to love him either. Then suddenly she remembered something else and pulled back from him. "The roast!"

"What about it?" Seth frowned.

"It's still in the oven." Abbie glanced at her watch. "Dinner is going to be ruined," she groaned.

"There will be plenty of other Sunday dinners," he assured her, and pulled her back into his arms where she belonged.